NOVEMBER

NOVEMBER

JARED WALSH

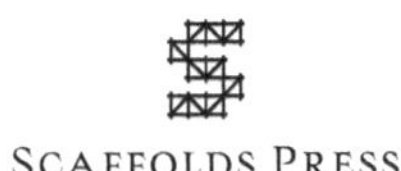

SCAFFOLDS PRESS

First Edition
Copyright 2024 by Jared Walsh

Manufactured in the United States of America

ISBN: 979-8-9915154-0-5

LCCN: 2024921576

For Mila, Lucia, and Leon.

ONE

"ANTONIA, BEGIN!"

Antonia, begin!

We live in an old landscape, the dreamy sort, the holy sort. The leaded glass windows of this house are warped into pregnant waves, and out them I see Polonius on the lawn smoking and waiting, he cannot stand the sweetness of my voice, it kills him. There is so much to say, we are overflowing with all this doing and undoing and there is no telling of it. It is autumn—

Polonius kicks the leaves. I see Polonius smiling. He cannot smile part of the way, his very skull distends, his hair bounces off his cheeks, his eyes close, and the wrinkles proliferate until his face is an animated bee-hive. He is remembering how he used to swim in leaves when he was small, and grope at the bottom matter to turn up the nature there. And he is projecting on the ribbed wall of the sky—the clouds are lining up

"

to be rolled into pastries and coated with raspberry preserves—the arc of our lives. We are gone—we are buoyed by the soft bellies of those clouds in a prismatic Paradise—yet we are closer to you than we ever could have been during our lives.

Polonius favors the less elegant side of a garden path, the bed where my rosemary is, and an apple tree holds its gauzy wings over an audience of radiant cabbage. Polonius' sky sits on the shoulders of what looks like arborvitae, it is actually an unusually erect grouping of Lombardy poplar. The poplars descend in close counterpoint from the two corners of the yard to the sycamores that tunnel the drive, and whose leaves swirl and regroup along the edges of the gravel.

How soon and how easily language fails me. I am too used to the five-act stage, and this is an actual stage, with no concrete clues. Antonia reminds me to take shelter in detail, that through the minute passages of thought and perception the threads of the high wire will be woven. And so.

There is the faint sense of train whistles in the air at night, which I don't mind, but Polonius hates—he says they remind him of Berlin, and he has spent whole days trying to swat away the sound. Streams bisect each other everywhere in the woods, and beyond that they meet again, the signatures of their infinite ways. When we are gone yet again, one of you will find the way here, and it will mean the world to me what words you engrave in the walls. There is a Roman forum buried under the sub-sub-basement of my mind. The password to the safe is INNISFREE.

The library is a Victorian tower discrete from the rest of the house, it is an island around which the stars turn with a special radiance, they bend their silver ears to hear my voice. I am connected to the cosmos by a vibrating string. I feel it pull on my heart, I feel it multiply and modulate the tone of my voice, I feel it drown the sorrows of generations in its brilliance, and one day there will be no song and no string and no canyon, and my mouth will be clasped shut, just as I began, before I went what the world calls crazy, I gave in to what the world calls genius, I became an echo of an echo, a shade of a shade, give me peace while I take a drink, there, now Polonius will approach. Antonia, no need, no need, please take a minute to yourself, the night will be so long.

TWO

—

"WE HAVE BEEN FIGHTING"

We have been fighting, thrashing for life and for death all at once, for the whole circle of existence. Not just in our minds, but with our bodies, with our flesh we have crushed and mauled and excoriated and worshipped and transfigured the circle. The beginning, the beginning, how did all this begin? Early on, before we knew what we were looking at, before we knew what signs to parse from others, the tulip from the labyrinth, the horse and the field of shaded snow from the depths of Velasquez, death, no, let me do it, *Death* came to us, to me and to November, in a dream in the form of a lover, or two lovers, and asked us why we kept rejecting her, or why we always embraced her only from behind and made her our human shield against life. Why not dance with her, say, and let her breathe her transposing fire into our mouths? What is more precious than the crystal yarn of a spider in the streetlamp or moonlight? I ask you.

God is not properly cared for in the Heavens. He forgets what he is doing, he has no one to play even chess with, he is killing the angels at rummy, at hearts, at shanghai, at bridge, spades, hi-low jack, at backgammon, and he has trouble, even with telescoping heat-seeking vision and oracles implanted in his immaterial skull, he has trouble finding a mate on Earth or otherwise to have simple intercourse or discourse with, an equal. The heavens are hellishly underpopulated, there are only two or three souls left, they say, and soon even they will be voted down, and it will be God and Michelangelo for the rest of eternity, staring at each other wondering who made whom. Plato is messing with Dante in a coldwater flat in Hell's Latin Quarter— Hell is the land of a thousand cities, where all the action takes place, but God can't get there. He is bored, so he sent Death down to us, to rig up some entertainment. He did not foresee how fully and fruitfully we would entertain *ourselves* with it.

In our library, there are three sets of spiral stairs linking three balconies, and in their oculus our voices flourish. Sometimes we are quiet as the ghosts that haunt this place and as delicate as starlings singing across the clotheslines of Lisbon; sometimes we bellow like animals, and our bodies seem to fill the whole cylinder of this space and the upper air, where the bells, if we had them, would caper and crash. I stand and speak to our daughter Antonia, who types on her typewriter—many of the letters are rubbed off the keys, and Antonia makes red annotations in the margins where her fingers have gone astray. Then, I imagine, November will come again, November will come while I sleep and while I wander the outside not standing the sweetness and eloquence of her voice because it will fill me with sadness and relieve me of the strength to do what we have promised each other we would do—November will come and elevate the page to her lips.

I am a teacher: after some moments spent fingering the grain of the pulpit's wood, I begin to preach. I shift, I jostle, I get carried away. Composition is uncomfortable. I would prefer to walk around the garden, to sit aside sphagnous fountains and feel the sun, to abuse and mutilate sticks by dragging them across the ancient rock walls. I would prefer to gather flowers and leaves and bugs from the underbrush and inspect them, my old friends, then throw them back.

THREE

"NOVEMBER IS SINGING"

November is singing, I do not want her to stop, I will go on.

My father was an Irishman, my mother was Portuguese. The two of them loved one another so much that they forgot to make money. We were raised in Brooklyn. Four brothers and six sisters, and one shower between us, one toilet, and one sink. We had to rise in the dead of night to do our business, and even so there was a line. For a month, close to the end, we lived off blubber scraped from a beached sperm whale at Rockaway and boiled with cans of creamed corn. When I finished high school, I left home with Anna Delancey. Together we traveled as far as we could imagine—to Philadelphia—where no one would be able to find us. Anna and I lived in the train yards, under the bridges, among the junk heaps and mountains of stone rubble, at home with the scrofulous muttering cranks who filled the air with their bewilderment like dead planets throwing off clouds of tears. We bathed in the mercurous Schuylkill, we stole our clothing from department stores, we begged our food from steakhouse kitchens, we performed acrobatics and dramas on the city squares, and we stole our happiness from the air itself. And we evolved. We educated ourselves gratis in the library of the University of Pennsylvania, and we found a corner of the stacks that had all but been left for dead, a lodge of Urdu or Sanskrit or some such inkblot language; the cleaning folk, whom I had come to despise for their knowledge of the special spots, had even abandoned the place. There Anna and I lived over winter, we fished our meals from the stackside trashcans, we cleaned ourselves delicately in the sinks. We embraced and slept in the purest darkness and silence that was left after the bells sounded the closing of the library and the last humming of the air ducts above us had evaporated and the souls were gone from the place, and the oscillation of the siren of human presence in our minds slowed to a wave, a whisper, and our own million ghosts, our armies of spirits and our private words, inscrutable to the world, started to gather round us as audience and the feeling of their breath on our necks was the feeling of the rising warmth of the earth.

Our existence rose to the most narrow and absurd of intellectual and spiritual heights. We spoke in secret tongues; our currency was poetry; our mother was Athena, our father Apollo—we were at once lovers and siblings. Our sadness, the miscellaneous sadness that afflicts one so sensitive to life, reached so far down along the taproot of our humanity that its extraction from our hearts felt as the mining of precious stones. Anna would cry uncontrollably when she was pushed over the edge of her private abyss, and the tears would fall down her cheek until she lay on a clouded mirror that trembled with the cadence of her sobs. I would try to touch her, and she would cringe and suffocate herself, luxuriantly, with her own despair. She would claw at me and she would say, Polonius, Polonius, I will die, I will die, that is alright, I do not mind, but I do not want you to die Polonius, I do not want you to die, and she would whisper it a thousand times until she slept. Then she would cry with every breath in her sleep, until the tongue of the gods dipped into the night and brought up the quicksilver of dawn, and still she would wheeze from behind her throat, from within the eyelet of her skull she would howl, until the tongue of the gods lapped up the darkness from its last hideaways, and we would emerge into the Sanskrit splendor of our bower and thank Arjuna or whomever it was that had brought us back to this life in this place.

The trouble came around the time when Anna began to give speeches in her sleep. She would hold forth with mystic clarity, not a somnolent pause or sigh would betray her state or muddle the logic, which was no logic, she was uttering those truths that do not obey the laws, she was pushing out the boundaries of the universe and describing what lay beyond intention. The trouble came because Anna began to sleep-lecture in a booming voice, and in time with the rise and fall of that voice was the ripple and crescent and snail of her body, a circle of contortions that made her mouth very hard to stop. Not that I wanted to stop her mouth, I wanted to give it a signal that its sage demagoguery had need of moderation. A hand was too suffocating, and my hands were not always clean. An arm she would bite. A book, pressed up against her lips with no greater force than a forefinger making a gentle cue of silence against one's own lips, placed a pillow under her voice so that the night janitor, a man so ugly that his footfalls would upend your stomach, would fail to go hunting in the stacks of Vishnu, which spooked him anyhow, after the barking coyotes of his hallucinations. I experimented with all possible shapes and thicknesses and orientations; there were several months in which the *Durnoi Encyclopedia of Philology* was my star. If I could cradle Anna onto her side, I could prop the *Durnoi* slightly against her mouth and it would hold there of its own weight. But then she told me, in the gray waking hours, Polonius, please do not try to feed me things while I sleep, I will not eat them or absorb them, and especially not this silly work on relations of words as if they have no life of their own. And this business of soul and sole and seul is really overworn. So, still silent on Anna's speeches, for I did not want them to cease, only to be contained, to me they were her apotheosis, I searched for something more to Anna's taste. Farrah Josephine was a joke. Yule Farber was too. I tried earnestly and failed more than a few times after that. And then I did not fail. *Animus Cognitus*, by T.E. Crowen Steam. It was a pamphlet bible of sorts, with a leather cover soft as kid gloves and soft binding and therefore soft pages. The book contained over one hundred thousand words of diamond edge that cut so clean that they slipped through my mind at first read—I understood nothing of the book—but Anna liked the feel of the cover against her lips, as if she were kissing the belly of a girl.

One morning, one blue and brilliant morning, let it be that, Anna draped herself onto a couch in a reading room and opened *Animus Cognitus* and began to know it from the inside. Her face cast shade, then a bird of recognition, and then a pearl of blinding submission and confluence with the work. I can imagine whole religions for which it would be a cardinal sin to look upon such a face. I spied over her shoulder, she shielded the page from me as if it were a final damning confession, I flew back into the stacks and found another copy, this one hard-bound and unbroken and stiff with years, and reread the book. I too began to feel the blood flow out of me onto the floor and be replenished from a spigot in the sky. On its surface, Crowen Steam's style imitated that of the continental philosophers of the last century, Isabella and Fernando in particular, and Role more subtly, imitated them so closely that his work appeared on its bejeweled surface some sort of forgery. I read and reread the first chapter. I scoured the stackside trash cans for a rejected tea, found it, returned. By this time Anna was at impossibly small intervals turning the pages, but still one by one, as if checking them for an earring or pin she had lost. I tried to catch up with her, but I was hooked and nearly shocked and put out of my lucidity by a line that had been underlined in pencil and annotated "preposterous!" in light cursive. It read,

There is no proof that an instant is not an hour, that a day is not a moment, that a lifetime is not a breath's time: so, who is to say that we do not proceed in a series of concentric ovals or chaotic doodles of time of immeasurable interval, and not in the circular fashion so drowsily advanced by the clock, or the progressive fashion so blithely advanced by History? If we cannot answer this question, then I might say in the same breath, and in the same truth, we are already dead and we will never die.

I saw in this thesis a theme that was produced and reproduced in a thousand forms throughout the work, a point that could not be proven or disproven, and therefore no thesis at all—and I circled the "preposterous" with my small finger, dabbed in the oversteeped tan of the tea. Anna, meantime, had perched the volume on her chest and was caressing it like a small animal. What? I asked her. I am done, she said.

That night Anna slept without a sigh, without a tear, without a whimper or howl, and without a pronouncement. I left her lying in perfect bliss, and then, starving as I had been all day, starved down past the skin of the bone and hung out to dry by the tea, composed my *Contra-Steam*. It was a rambling work, a raging work, yet it was the theoretical basis for all my future philosophical projects and the forge for a thousand swords: the simple statement that time is a continuum, your death is not yet here but it will come, you cannot prepare, and it will matter more than anything you have ever done: It will end you and everything else. Time is on the road to nowhere.

What you let unfold next, god or gods, I will not forgive, no matter how many times I imitate you. I took up my scraps of paper and folded them in my coat; I showered in the sink; I returned to our Sanskrit walls—to a void. No Anna was there. I searched through the reading rooms, the bathrooms, the halls and the stacks and the carrels. I risked all and called for her. The night janitor was set in motion; I moved to escape. Out on the street the night was bitter winter, there was ice falling from the sky, there was no one in the streets. I ran in all directions, I circled the library in all its tremendous and meaningless bulk, and at the end of my energy a hedge shook in the distance along the walls of a lonely courtyard, and a running spot of darkness shot into the street. I followed the darkness, it hied away from me, and with my heart now losing the will to propel me, I saw Anna run out of the campus and into the nothingness that swirled over the Schuylkill River. From far behind her I reached out to her, I cradled her face in my hands, I tried to tell her how priceless, how irreplaceable . . . how I adored her, would put down my pen and my very mind for her, would turn myself into a noodling tripe of misery for her. I tried, she did not hear, she flew out onto the old South Street bridge that used to span the river at just enough height to create chaos, I saw her throw her book over the parapet before her, and gasping helplessly her name I saw her follow it, down.

A voice spoke to me at that moment when Anna passed from view and from life, concomitant with her hawk's treble lament and the slap of her body against the surface of the river. The voice spoke from my inner mouth to my inner ear, the safe that only opens for a single utterance and shuts that utterance in for all eternity. The voice told me, Polonius, you are alive. We locked eyes, I and I, and I saw the fires leap and hurl from the abyss between water and sky, the madness of Polonius was outmaneuvered by Polonius, and the smoke from the fires coagulated into a death mask that hovered above the water. This is the end, said the mask, of your bodily existence. You have known total loss— now you are free. Now you inhabit the world.

FOUR

—

"WHAT IS TRUTH?"

What is truth? We all must find out for ourselves, and as Polonius and I will say many times during this parade of illumination, the thing we seek to define is not a thing at all. When you arrive at our degree of experience, nothing can be equated with anything else. We do not say, this is this. We say, this is not this and not that, and just as a planet is born from the negative space of the universe, a vision of ecstatic reality starts to take shape.

Truth for us—. We did not find that life took us in warmly, as into a club, or offered us sustenance. Our path has been a grueling, near-blind pursuit of something by its nature unattainable, and the pursuit has yielded us, like the sun in the eyes of the Poet, views of the tectonic geography of our souls. Are we limitless? Are the earth and sky limitless? What about their union at the horizon? I do not know if that is the right question, but I have been nearer to the horizon than I ought to have been, I have been tongue to tongue with the sun, and the closeness melted the rice paper from off my eyes—I spied on our lonesome God as he reached down from his cloudy perch and plucked the pendulum of life from the breast of one man and pressed the bronze weight of existence into the hand of another. Down here on earth we have the strong sense that no question has an answer, and that sense feels like futility, but out there, out at the tail ends of existence, we knew—

I grew up in the countryside of western Pennsylvania, where my father farmed the same tract of land granted to his ancestors by William Penn. As a child, I spent early mornings walking wooded paths in strobe-like shade with my mother, her eyes and hands fatigued from her long nights at the piano. Beside us, behind us, all around us were the sounds of the Clarion River, I hear its flow against the stillness of the ashes and oaks, behind the sharps and cries of the birds, through the waves of memory that lift and drop the spirit in time to the beating of my heart. I see my mother in the dawn asking her maid to arrange a band of astromeriad silk around her miniature ears, we will go into the forest before the frost drops from the leaves—or we will go in the vengeful moment of summer, when the cows stand with their tongues plastered to their chests hoping to catch a tear from their own eyes. Before dawn the whole world was Picasso's blue. On the way to the schoolhouse, my mother, the schoolmistress, in front of me, her sole student, would light her first cigarette, and the clouds she made would hang like moss in the branches above us and form mist mirrors for the rising day, and she would rest half-way down the path on a granite bench that she had built exactly for the purpose. The schoolhouse was the warming room of a ten-horse barn. My desk was a repurposed tack table. My couch was the divine trainer's couch. My mother taught me all she knew, and when she ran out of her own knowledge, we read the histories and the great works together. I would swim back and forth through the pages, I was a compulsive non-finisher of books, I did not want to give their images permission to leave, and if I hit the end of one accidentally, I would throw in a mark somewhere in the middle, so that when I returned to the book some months later, I would believe that it still bordered me with its luxuriance on all sides. Every afternoon, after my cup of coffee boiled over the hearth to a chalk brown and adulterated with sugar just to the precipice of sweetness, I would take a siesta on the couch. I would feel my own weight wash against the insides of my fingertips and cloy there, energy and fatigue would eddy in my thighs until they both drained out my spine, while the daydream, in my half-sleep, would intensify and mingle with the sound of my mother lighting a match.

If there was time in the dusk, my father and I hunted bear, deer, badger, raccoon, fox, and all others whose eyes glowed at us from the undergrowth. We fell in with the untold rhythms of the forest, we felt the branches close and open doors in the woods and indicate our ways, we took our horses down the avenue-broad trotting paths from which, from above, the whole wood hung like a giant sycamore leaf from its thread, and its veins were the matrix we made with our bloodthirsty meanderings. You can die of anything, Cherry November, my father would say, each time as if it were the first, and each time removing his cap as if he were in the presence of a deity built from the tones of his own voice, you can kill with anything too, this gun could be a knife, it could be a stone, it could be a hand, it could be a bottle, it could be loneliness, drink, trampling, exposure, heat or cold, hunger or gluttony, you can die from life itself, but the hunter, to the extent that he is willing to kill, he is willing to die, and he is not afraid, his act derives from an abundance of peace in his heart, of quiet strength as powerful and constant as the turning of the earth in space. The hunter is entirely immersed in the present moment, for nature knows no future, it is continual disorder, and man—(he always said *man*, and it made my whole body tingle, to be classed with the Khans)—man is not the eye of this storm, he is out among the rogue waves on the back edges of the vortex, and he must balance atop those waves.

We had a storage barn converted to a standstill preserve of every beast we had killed in the pose we could last remember: the coyote shot trying to howl a possum alive; the sow showing her rage at our approach of her cubs; the fox in lazy disbelief; ten or twenty stunned deer—of which there was a particular buck, my favorite, with a neck too turgid for its head, and with brute mass nearly surging out its black eye. He was my first kill. I shot him on the run, when his body was at its most extreme tension, and the life exploded from his body as he tumbled in the leaves. We gutted him there, his face was half alive still, not yet vacant, the blood poured out deep as a wine cask, it poured out even after I reached inside of him and unhooked his heart from its hangar and threw it to the buzzards, the wisest and most majestic of birds, I would never shoot a buzzard even if it were to save my life, those sacred messengers of the skies, those connoisseurs of the afterlife, they cradle me in their narrowing circles, their arc is my arc, their dive is my dive, their swarm my swarm, their rise my rise—if I were not so intent on a silent death I would let them pull me apart just as loneliness pulled apart the poet who sang the dismemberment of Orpheus by the nymphs. When I die, Antonia, lay me out in the field.

After a kill my father would call for his enormous manservant Johnno with three blasts on an absurd miniature of a hunting horn he had found in the window of a children's bookstore in Erie, a horn that sounded like the amplified distress of a woman whose dress has caught its hem in a printing press, not so much a signal that she would be crushed between the drums as that the dress or the paper was ruined. Johnno defended our backs from earthbound scavengers while we gutted our kill, sewed tight the wound, and wrapped the carcass in a tarp for loading on Johnno's bloodsmirched cart drawn by Otium, a horse, whose bouncing strides were punctuated with suspicious sniffs over his shoulder, and Otium would put on speed to outrun the plume of carnage that dogged him, so that Johnno, driving the cart with erect ceremony up the long fold that wreathed the farmhouse and garden, appeared to my reading and smoking and waiting mother as a black Ajax storming her leisure. We would collect our wandering horses from the wild raspberry and baby grasses nursing under the aegis of juniper shades, we would follow hot after Johnno, and we would hear him utter, through an igneous armor of restraint, and with closed lips so that the sound seemed to pipe from his ears, a high howl of conquery and joy and half madness, which we would answer, my father first, with war screams that would have hurled Johnno from his driver's seat were he not so acutely expecting them.

In the darkness, I wrote dramas and convinced my parents to act them out for whomever were our guests that night—the guest wing was semi-permanent housing for distant relatives, bankrupts, artists, writers, producers, and divorcees, who would invite themselves at what must have been calculated intervals to wander for hours in the fields and finger the brushstrokes in the portraits and turn over and over the lead-heavy silver knives—and for these guests we resurrected the death of Cicero, the exile of Ovid, the battle of Ain-Jalut, the argument of Regina v. Dudley and Stevens, the night before the Crucifixion, all with skull shattering irony, and one guest, a novelist who had written an unreadable series concerning what would happen if one sat in a theater so long that one's soul became an actor, reported contracting the hiccoughs for the entire following week, leading to a series of migraines that culminated in a bout of drinking lasting sixteen years, during which he produced a single work—a boozy one but rightfully recognized as a comic masterpiece concerning the mortal dangers of sitting too long at bus stations. That work earned him the Nutting Prize. The writer did not forget my role in his beatification: the frontispiece of *Integrals* hangs framed in my dressing room, inscribed with the words, "To the one who made me wish there were no such thing as laughter."

Alongside the writer's homage hangs a watercolor of Turnberry Hall, mounted on a flamboyant sextet of wooden boards and bearing the inscription, *ornata est.* I was sent to Turnberry at thirteen, dwarfed by my violin, and four years later, after a summer at the Berliner Conservatory, I left home again for the University of Pennsylvania and the Curtis Institute. By this time I had declared my true love for my mother's true love, that most voluptuous of stringed instruments, the piano. The keys had become my orchestra and audience, the body of the piano became my body, the strings of the piano were my sinews and my scribes. If I could not act as I wanted, at least I could leave my hands to their own devices, to caper and masquerade, to dance in formations that the mind did not need to understand. There are infinite layers of silent music behind the birdsong of the piano, layers whose melody and key are not quantifiable and will not play antiphon to any other— therefore will not sound to the ear, will only sound to the body in its inexplicable shifts and movements, and express themselves in the tremble of the fingers that gives life to the music in the first place. In those years, I needed no communal existence beside that with my own self, I wanted for no friend or lover or protector, I wanted for no one.

My home in Philadelphia was a Romanesque town-house built by my grandfather to house his mistresses and a herd of servants. The last tenant of the house had been Alexandra Nouvelle, an opera singer with a mysterious relation to my mother that my parents called cousin. Alexandra had left an echo of her taste on the limewashed marble of the reading table, a copy of Lloyd Dennis' *Porous Vex* eagled by an unbreached apple long turned to perfume and monumented by a silver coffee urn banded with a frieze of what appeared to be tophatted elephants. Shunning the main bedrooms for their emptiness, she had made her home on the secretive top floor, whose deep velvet walls and impenetrable midnight drapes and teacups stained with the ink of wine and plaster-encrusted drawing room with a well-played piano and furniture on bestial stilts, portholed and doubled everywhere by round mirrors bearing the golden fires of the Sun King, spoke to me of the heady leisure of my grandfather and the wild drunken loneliness of the opera singer. On the top floor I too settled, and the faces of the mirrors kept me company, faces of distress, of longing, of hilarity, of boundless absurdity, of terror, of surprise, of vanity, of searching for something in the imaginary background, of searching for something in my own face that would disappear as soon as it were discovered, immortality, or lack of bounding by my physical boundaries, the face's very absence, or its omnipresence in the world and the universe, the idea of November as unlaced as the wind that gave sudden gravity to the room—for weeks I swanned freely in myself and in my eternal cup of reboiled coffee and the smoke of an eternal cigarette and the smack of sugar on my lips there, and in a single line of poetry lying innocent in a crumbling octavo on the violet couch, innocent of the fact that it had sparked me so violently that I would need a lifetime to descend to the floor and read another; I swanned in the single stroke of a finger on the out-of-tune piano that sent me wafting through storm and portents of the Caribe in a plume of starlight caught in the hazy eye of the captain, two-five-nine leagues from Norman running with a heady gale, and all his crew in mutiny though he sailed alone.

A long way of saying, if I hoped to read what the long beards of Pennsylvania would have me read, and if I hoped to compose something apart from my whirling dervish marginalia, I needed to reach the University library. On the landing of the top floor of my house there grazed an inexplicable bicycle. I discovered a service elevator behind the mirror image of the door to my petit foyer, and rode with the bicycle down five stories on that magic carpet. Thus I and my weighty Peugeot made it out into the street, day after day, and then most deliciously night after night, when the streets basked in the many-flavored silences of the city, and the sky over the river played echo chamber and shadow globe to the purpureous manes of the winds.

On the night Anna's soul opened a doorway in the river to be drowned, I wore a thick woolen cape, the steam of my exertions flowed out the hood into the howling freeze, and out the back of me, I imagined, trailed a ruby fire. On my mind was a vague waltz, on whose parquet a single couple dances, back to back.

FIVE

"ANNA DELANCEY COULD NOT SWIM"

Anna Delancey could not swim. She could have waded with me in the murky waves at Brighton, but Anna preferred, when she did go with me down that broad empty boulevard to the ocean, the Russian pickle shops and pickled cabbage vendors and tiny bookstores whose inscrutable texts were written on rice paper no thicker than the wrappings of the prune-filled chocolates sold at their counters; she preferred to wait for me under the dripping subway trestle, whose shade occupied a quiet after the storm of a train that had passed, and she would relate to me the terror of those rickety reverberations in thunderous eloquence as I rearranged my sopping, chafing khakis, my only pair of pants and my worst. I tried to teach her to swim in the community pool, where far more than imaginable other people who could not swim would congregate to spit water; I tried to teach her in a stream that gathered all manner of sputum for its transit to Sheepshead Bay; I tried to teach her in an iridescent puddle, in a dream; she would not go; even the sound of a running bath would draw a claim of high treason; yet I used to catch her, late in the library night, drawing a sink full of water and watching her fingers twirl and dive into the miniature spring and frolic along its pearly banks, and I would remark to myself that she wished the miracle of buoyancy to remain a miracle, never to walk the gangplanks of reality.

So Anna dropped from the South Street bridge and from existence, and I straddled the parapet, my hands and chest open to the wind, my teeth rattling like the talk of cormorants in my skull. The snow flew upwards at me from the purple face of the river in turbulent gusts. Paralyzed with terror, with sadness, with the unspeakable, I spoke to myself from beyond feeling, I spoke brute reason: symmetry: we would die one, then the other, therefore occupying for ever and ever facing pages in life's book, facing carrels in the stacks of Hell, facing fate-lines in the two hands of the deity—provided that I could cause myself to strike the water at an abominable angle. I stood up on the wall. An itch, far worse than any bodily itch you might imagine, arose and burned in the small of my soul's back, and it begged, it winged, it whimpered, it moaned—the itch was for weightlessness, for the ecstasy of being unlocked from its cage and set loose, for the play it would have with other souls, for the million limbs it would use to scratch all of its itches—

My flight took me down into a puddle of darkness that grew in comfort and serenity and silence. I took the night into my mouth; I shook my head in a kind of self-mockery; I closed and opened my eyes; I flailed and found that it did no good; then, a crescendo of violence very nearly tore my head away from its root. I was enlivened and frozen stiff at once, and my body was cast into a meditative trance of suffering—no foolish thoughts of eternity now—in a solitary room there was I, and there was, filling the same space, the earthen red wallpaper of pain. At the deepest cul de sac of numbness, when I ought to have let myself drift past the hemicircle of light and into the woods as a dog would, to die, I made a move, I stretched out my arms and legs, as if to give an asterisk to my life—and I began to float to the surface.

I could not move, the river was too cold, so I floated on my back and wondered. I wondered, waited and watched. I was being carried under the bridge by the current, I remember thinking, it would be pleasant to die under the shelter of the bridge, whose underside was painted a convenient black. Then the sky opened up into a million playful swarms of ice crystals running and pausing in the night like felines or silent movie actresses, and I saw the angel of the underworld swan dive over me. The way she grew in proportion with the cool violet flame of the sky made me think, perhaps I was rising into Hell, as in a parody of apotheosis, and then, quickly, matters of metaphysics were put off by the need to stop lying there like a target. She came down entirely without spotting her landing, her head was tucked down between her arms, and her body made a strident whisper in its descent as the whirring of a hummingbird's wings. I thrashed—I could not thrash—all had gone cold. She hit the water with terrible force not an arm's length from my head, and I can still hear the scream she let go when she popped up, all wet as an otter and joyous, a scream that trains make when they are sure of having lost their brakes down a mountain face. She tried to cradle me, but I was too lumberlike; so she took me by the hair and dragged me across the river to the stony bank where I had once lived. She laid me on the rubble of the shore and ran up the embankment to the bridge and returned stark naked and stripped me equally, laid a black woolen cape over me with the delicacy of someone handling a newborn for the first time, careful to tuck the edges under my bluing body, and made as if to return to the river— for Anna.

With all the strength in me I took my savior by the hand. I called out to her, I could not, my voice had frozen, so I told her with my eyes, she was not going back in the river. Anna Delancey was dead.

In my gaze there must have been present too, not so much the folly of desire, not the tragicomedy of lust, these are masks for what lies beneath, and in that moment I was all beneath—there must have been present the sickness of knowledge of our identity, that this angel of the underworld was I and I she, that I felt as my own her immortal vigor, that her vigor was now my vehicle. Her body, its embodiment of me, loomed over me, legs all aquiver, arms all aquiver, it waited, as you might wait in the danger of a field to see if the lightning would take you, and yes, and yes, I reached out for her, I was warming to life again, and I overpowered her and caught her up in my arms before the hummingbird flew again, before Persephone could make her way back home, I pulled her down against me for a moment, until she stirred. She struggled against her own instincts, she clawed the ground as if the earth were coal-bright sky from which she had fallen, a dark moon whose gravity she had lost, and her body shook with the frustration of a pathological sinner who is erroneously committed to the organ concerts and lawn tennis of Paradise—but I had her now by my arms, which I bound up around her and whose bond she could not break.

Draped in our clothing and trailing the Peugeot and hooded by the cape like two apes of a monstrous circus animal and even laughing, we ran back to November's house near the square, which at the time was so needlessly opulent that I felt I was in a highly underserved version of the afterlife. We sighed and groaned a million sighs and groans of relief as we sank into the hot water of two parallel bathtubs, mine the one with raven's claws and hers the one with sorcerer's hands, and I lay in the water with my head showcased on a silver satin pillow under archers who threatened each other with cupidinous pains and formed with the trajectories of their arrows a star in the ceiling fresco. I slept, the spirit approached, the two doors to the bathroom swung apart revealing a perfectly naked and perfectly oiled Persephone, and I awakened enough to tell that her body was moving my way with some purpose, I could smell it on her skin. I raised a lazy hand to give a sign of pause and explained that part of me still needed time to gather itself. She took the hand, split the fingers, placed them on her chest and said, I am Cherry November.

SIX

"THE THEORETICAL IDENTITY"

The theoretical identity of our senses with ourselves gives us the illusion of truth, the illusion of control. I see, I feel, I taste, I hear, I smell, I know, I remember.... But I do not do these things, the transitive is a lie, we simply do not have language to express how life invades us. The steam of my exertions ... a ruby fire. The steam of my exertions ... a ruby fire. The steam of my exertions ... a ruby fire. Every night of my afterlife, my body levitates on the steel momentum of my Peugeot, my lips are sugared with numbness, my vision receives orbs and waves of purple light from behind a gauzy screen of ornaments, my hands pulse the brakes for the sensation of tension and forgiveness. Every night comes Anna, and the sound of her body against the water echoes against the moaning sides of the buildings. Every night comes Polonius and the transfiguring cold of the river—the water itself a prismatic quicksilver of darkness—my breath stolen from my chest as quickly as it was stolen from Anna's. Every night I return to the moment when I felt the weight of terror and disbelief at the finality of her act—the moment I nearly perished from empathy—the moment Anna's slipstream dragged me with her.

You earthlings enjoy imagining that you will reunite with your doting uncle, or with your rabid yet sensitive mother, or god forbid with your dog, in the sunny hereafter. This is true. But it is not true in the way one used to believe. I do not imbibe ambrosia with Bismarck and Karenin; I do not recline on foggy tufts with Steinbeck or Sinatra. Time does not work this way. It does not "keep going" until it reaches an "end", where everyone is gathered up and distributed according to their worth or deeds; Time does not have anywhere to be. Rather, Time doubles and triples back on itself, even extending beyond its original range in either direction. Sometimes it breaks out of all relativity, and there passes a durée not unlike a transoceanic voyage, and sometimes it gets itself tangled in tiny curlicues no larger than a paperclip. Time is an organism of infinitely inclusive curiosity. It will crane its neck around a continent in order to listen to an original melody . . . and it will traverse generations to discover a body, a warmth, a pair of hands. I wish that I

could tell you I witnessed Anna devoured by the har-
pies of the seventh circle. I wish that I knew the result
of her act. I wish there were indeed a goal, an end, to
all this, even if it be a gory end or one turned treacle
with bathos. But there is no Hell, there is no Dis, there
is no Paradise, there is no moving on from this. Dante is
still pining for Beatrice. Agamemnon is still mourning
Iphigenia. Women and children are still being inciner-
ated in Hamburg and Dresden. Mozart is still hacking
it in Mannheim. Picasso is still mourning the incessant
din of doves and cranes at Cannes. Hemingway is still
boxing his own ears in Idaho. Hannibal is still camp-
ing out by Tarentum. Mao is still scheming at his tent
capital. A warrior monk is still twisting the knife in his
own bowels. Ovid is still dreaming of his homecoming.
Anna is still holding forth in her sleep, her cheek all
but fossilized in a pool of tears. Your parents are still
expecting you. And you are still in that infinite period
before your birth.

SEVEN

"A BRILLIANT CONCOCTION"

A brilliant concoction of study and fraud inducted me into the class of 1973 at the University of Pennsylvania. November studied music and theatre with a band of communists and stoned saints, and I studied philosophy under the stars of Nietzsche and Kierkegaard and all their faithful footmen. We lived in November's house of mirrors, we kicked and screamed and fucked and danced and made ourselves into babies again, we sat wasted and naked and breathed into each other's mouths, we read out loud to each other Brockden Brown, Polybius, Miller, the Russians, Rosetti, Woolf, Camus, Maturin, Beckett, Ovid, Blake, and Borges, and every night I cradled her in my arms and fell asleep with her weight on top of me.

We met Federico on the college green one night. He was holding open a copy of *The Silver Dove*, and Biely was one of our Russians. Federico or I needed a cigarette. Next morning I woke up to the laughter of November and three nameless girls trying to locate their underpants in a chaos of sheets and sweat. I went down to the kitchen and found Federico with an icepack to his forehead and his cock looking a bit worse for wear.

"I could do that again," he said.

November, that omnivore, devoured everything we brought home to her. We were one and the same blood from the beginning, losing one another would have been impossible, possession was impossible, so too was jealousy. Maybe you do not understand, maybe you have never felt what I mean, and I do not begrudge anyone their innocence.

All the while a tune played under the current of our lives, a musical one, a poetic one, alternating, radiating, harmonizing. I began to write *The World Meter*.

Desire is what keeps up alive. I am not only talking about desires that land you on the moon. I am talking about desires that sail you through a moment. If you watch us from above, we never seem to be too creative with these. It is food, or it is fuck. But think of the multitude of women, or men. Lovely, ugly, middling. Think of how you ought to touch them. Think of how you want to, how they want you to. Some with your eyes, some deep up in the northwest quadrant of the insides, some with your teeth on the arm, some with the back of your hand, some not at all, phantoms, they want to be set apart. Add to this, the mind may dream of many women and men at once, it only remains to let go our fear of failure. Think of the experiences in which you could indulge, if you were to cast off the ideal of "happiness" or "contentment". Is smiling stasis to be enjoyed? Why do you think clowns are so terrifying?

Think of the multitude of women . . . eyes, insides, teeth, hands, phantoms.

November on the piano and Federico on the guitar, myself as mouthpiece, we were minstrels and mad philosopher kings who wanted no followers. We took in Jesuits, Jews, Jehovah's Witnesses, Yellows, Blacks, Reds, Pinks, and Coffees. It was especially delicious to turn a prudent girl into one's sex slave. Rose was the first. She was a Catholic, and resisted us for six weeks. I was patient, November was noncommittal, Federico was outright nonplussed. He called her a termagant, a virago, a fishwife. He invited her out to the Paris Club and chaperoned Vishna, our little belly dancer, at the same time. It was an important night. The Paris Club in its day was walled in red velvet and shaped in a gyre with bars on all floors and in all corners, especially if you sat at the bar the entire time and never left. The dance floor likewise was everywhere, and if you took cocaine, the bathroom was everywhere. I was with Elise, a Spanish Mexican white and soft and strong, and November brought Diego, a Panamanian whom we had never seen before or since. Everyone danced with someone they didn't know, and at the end of the night Rose was left outside next to an English girl with a hook for a hand and the rest of us went home with a core of Chinese violinists. They remarked in the over-crowded taxi that they could no longer listen to music . . . we whisked them upstairs where November turned out dithyrambs of Prokoviev on the piano and we all fucked the violinists until the scene went black.

On the seventh week, just past the point where we had lost all hope, Rose walked into November's house and stripped off her clothes.

Rose had the palest of nipples and the blackest of eyes. Nation-building and security and diplomacy and legislatures and foundations. She wrote letters to soldiers. She crusaded for the cure of this or that dis-ease. She adopted children in Africa, sent them allow-ances, sent them rice and milk and antibiotics. She prayed for everyone in a plaster trance. She continu-ally insisted that her anus be attended to, even when other holes were not occupied, probably out of some sort of misplaced piety. She had a prejudice against girls, one that November solved by strapping on a long pink prosthetic that still tasted like November's last experience, and slapping Rose's face with it until Rose asked to be penetrated.

Rose had a way, during the daytime, of never speaking of what she did during the nighttime. Talk of love and love making was foreign to her, when pressed she insisted on her lifelong celibacy, and denied that she had ever set foot in our bedrooms or would ever again. To her the unspeakable nature of sex made the act worthwhile in the first place. There is a thrill to desperation, to hunger, to failure, to loss. The feeling of the ground trucking up to meet you. There is a thrill, gentle but lasting, to self-denial. Just as I refuse to recount my entire life in one sentence—and that constant refusal, that putting-off of the inevitable, twists this narrative into a certain shape—Rose twisted herself into a curiosity by means of a deity who called always for the exclusion of some course from her meal. She may have been miserable, but that was the point. Misery was her indulgence. Let go of this ideal of happiness, which is not a thing.

The mendicant cannot be said to be brainwashed. His inheritance of tradition is no evidence of blindness. There are traditions for all of us to inherit, be we atheists, cooks, salesmen, thieves. For each there is the idea that what he does carries some nobility, however finite. Even the one who decides he will disappear in an untrodden wood: the painter, the professor, the explorer.

The mendicant is not "repressed." Nor is anyone. Repression implies that there is some universal tune that plays, and those whose ears are not open, or who refuse to hear, are guilty of some sort of self-wrong. But wrong how? There are no real judges of actions on earth. There is only life and death, and not living and not dying. And we don't even begin to understand the nature of these two things.

Our association with Rose lasted through college. I credit her with the tuning of a sexual endurance among us that rivals the tantric monks. As lightning over the ocean during a strobelike storm, the thunderclap of climax shot through her body at tight and stochastic intervals, and whoever at those nearly infinite moments was lovelocked with her would be struck with monstrous energy. Late into the night and early into the morning, her cries and her seizures roiled and crashed, the tether of reality was loosed, the walls of our cave danced with a silhouette in which no one could be parsed from any other.

At the end we lay wasted and banged out and self-disgusted on the floor for a long time having to piss badly but too thirsty to move. Through the membranes of delirium there would seep the laughter of anticipation, laughter of indulgence, laughter through tears of laughter. Laughter at ourselves, in irony and in earnest. Laughter at Saint Peter on the way up, or down. Laughter at our nakedness—so simple, so absurd, and so complete. Why had it taken us so long to get back to the state in which we were born? We have been here on earth all this time, waiting, waiting, talking, talking...

Kant on the categorical imperative, Kant on the objectification of people. The man was struck, intellectually, by lightning, but instead of lending his mind a boisterous spark, the fateful bolt left him charred and dull. No action is repeatable, whether it be in a thought experiment or a life experiment. Kant's command that we do things as we would have them done, if they could be repeated throughout the world—this is a recipe for nothingness, and you and I even do "nothing" in different ways... We are all subjects and objects, whether or not we think it proper. Our lives form a proposition, and that proposition, as a far better philosopher so quietly observed—the proposition is articulate.

I remember certain nights, I can taste them and feel them and turn them over and over in the machinery of my mind. Take a scene at the Ruse, a French bar serving Argentine wines, in the breezy ecstasy of late summer. November, myself, Federico, and Rose. November was sitting Indian-style on a barstool, in a Columbian blouse with midnight eyeliner under her eyes. She drank wine with her teeth, which always came away stained like virgin cloth, while she read from my prized copy of *Either/Or.* She made a hundred million miniscule silent remarks with her eyes and mouth while perched there prominently on the bar stool in the manner of a parakeet. Her voice rang out,

"He is so prescient to have written a thousand pages on the theme of seducing a woman. Seduction is the thrill to all existence. The aftermath is just mechanics. Life does have a demonic and probably perverted taste for foreplay. All theatre art is foreplay, I haven't seen a production yet that treats of one's existence after marriage, or murder."

" The playwrights were too young to know of either."

"The end of philosophy. What happens after the end of philosophy?"

"Somehow I have it in my head that the opposite of a philosopher is a person who does not like the smell of his own shit."

"I do spend a long time in the bathroom, in the shower though. I would live underwater, if I could. I went to grade school with a girl who devised a waterproof book. It had cellophane on the pages. I am still in love with her. But I know that she is wasted somewhere, and fat as a dirigible."

"The girl you were in love with was probably yourself, you just didn't have any way to know. You will have to use Rose to make up for all the things you missed."

"Rose."

Rose turned to us and wiped to one side the hair that was pasted in her eyes. She was crying with laughter. Federico was making faces at her. A sheep's face. An ass's face. A mole's face. A terrapin's face. A ghost's face. A horror face. A referee's face. A face without description. Faces of dreams where you find yourself on a plane that will not make the landing. The more portentous the faces became, the more insatiate Rose's laughter grew. She bent her whole body into the pursuit. Federico, still locked in an expression of mock desperation, started kissing those tears.

At this point the needle skips, and I see myself with the three of them outside the bar. November has one hand in my pocket fishing for a match, and the other deposits a cigarette between my teeth. Her mouth hangs just slightly open. Freckles swim about her nefarious green eyes. "Where are you taking us, Polonius?"

"If I knew it wouldn't be worth taking anyone."

"I had a quiet life, before this, Polonius," she said.

"Do you want it back?"

She shook her head.

"Not even a little bit?"

"Not even a little bit."

That night none of us got any sleep. We fucked each other into oblivion, and in the dawn we fucked each other back into existence. In the late morning I lay next to a dozing November and feathered my fingertips over her body and promised myself that if the gods were ever going to take her back, they were going to take me too.

In the thing all possibilities concerning that thing are contained. This is a tautology, but a useful one: we are what we are. If this proposition does not scare you, then gargle yesterday in the pit of your soul...

Psychology, Philosophy, History, and even Literature are too lazy to map the human soul. They identify nebulae, and perhaps a galaxy or two, without ever drawing close enough to the planets to claw in vain through entire worlds of gas and dust and admit that they emerge with desperate empty hand, and the memory of ineluctable gravitation.

The days were winched up the slope with espresso, shot through with cigarettes, fluffed up with cocaine, shelved and quaking to the hilt with art, blessed and cursed by the sun and the moon, licked and scorched by dreams, and annihilated by the nights. Composition came early and easy, in nauseous spurts—Federico on the easel and later the music sheets, I at the type-writer, November at her piano—each to share with the other and evoke the word after which there was nothing to be said.

Self-expression has been hailed as the great triumph of modern psychology, but it is not for everyone. Some of us will pull musical notes out of our mouths. Others will pull their guts clean free of their bearings. Still others will have no idea what they have done.

On the bad nights, Federico and I would come home empty and shattered to find November standing on her head and practicing lines of Shakespeare in the presence of Elise, who was far more beautiful than your fantasy of her, and who had come home with us the night of the Cantonese violinists and stayed. A teapot always wheezed on the stove, the place was always rich with smoke.

"You are an impossibly peaceful creature November."

(Wiggling her toes) "Anything is possible, Polonius."

EIGHT

"I LIVED AS A BIRD"

I lived as a bird floating on the graces of the crests and cradles of the air and sea, whereas Polonius was a diver, he clawed for electric eels in the canyons, and seven thousand fathoms of pressure howled in his ears. The mornings, my soft children, were wretched premature births for him, with vampire bats waking up in his guts and black horse rodeos beginning in his brain. His heart was shocked and impaled by the ray of sunlight and would seem to want to crawl back into the womb of sleep, where people and places he knew were transformed into the scaffolding for works of art. The world to him was a drab mock-up of the dream. The world to me was an amplification and vivification of the dream.

On that grey and literary morning of the day I am still living, a day I could spend the rest of my life telling you about, the streets were strung out and empty. Polonius and I sat together in my room around the bubbler, a giant blue glass smoke balloon, on a carpet strewn with sooty wine glasses and bottles, with cutouts of eyes and heads from magazines, with sheet music and theatre scripts and ladies' underpants and puzzle pieces, with the morning's coffee pot and cups and those of many mornings before, with a Columbian flag I was knitting, with papers and tobacco and stems and seeds, and what could have been thousands of books and notebooks and manuscripts and notes and little pieces of paper with something written on them in my noodling cursive or Polonius' scribble. The rain hovered in the air and quested about. Polonius started talking.

"I spend more time in sleep than ever. I try to revisit certain dreams. The words in dreams seem to have more meaning than they ever could in real life. The words. For example. Last night. We were all on a train. We were not on the train as normal but on top of it, on the roof, and there were guards around us on the ground seeming ready to kill us if we got off. The train was traveling at an incredible speed, and I looked at you and you could barely hold on. Somehow I could not reach you, so I went to the conductor and asked him if he could stop it, and he said yes, but we would die if we hit the ground. And I said to him, November cannot hold on, so you need to stop the goddamn train. He said to me: *you get one shot at this.* Then he pulled a lever and the thing came to a halt, and we were cast into a field with dogs and tiger-headed people walking them, huge colonnades of trees, some kind of weird Arcadia of life. We were dragged along by this tide of wonderment, of mirabilia, like children who are seeing everything for the first time. We were holding hands, you and I, but we had lost control over our bodies. Yes. The feeling of losing control was the most valuable. Losing control without fear. While we were on the train, you could call the train 'life', I had this metallic taste of fear in my mouth, as if I could not prevent my mind from falling through the basement of its expectations. Horror, even, horror surrounding the idea of undergoing experience, no matter how trivial, of being separated from you in time or space or otherwise, the horror of impending death that can only be solved by death. I wonder, how can we transcend the unknown, how can we live both here on earth and in the realm of Arcadia?"

As you might expect, I took a long draw from the giant blue glass smoke balloon, then when nothing came to mind after that I took a good few more. I poured us two semi-generous glasses of wine in the least besmirched glasses I could find, and I lit two cigarettes, as was the fashion back then if you were lighting one. After all this fogging and heightening of the mind I came out with:

"How big is the mouth of your soul, and how open are the ears? The soul is the only thing in you that can speak, and it is the only thing that truly listens. So you have to cultivate both faculties. Maybe you are trying to tell yourself something that your waking soul won't hear. We are alive, we love each other, in the way that there is no word other than love that captures it so clearly. That I know is true. What else is true? What else is there? I believe that the greater parts of us, the highest and best parts and also the most compelling parts, the parts that make us alive, would not exist if they could be put into words. I think dreams are the music, not the notes and not the words, the raw music of our insides, and from time to time that music merges with the greater river of imagination and experience, the two inseparable as the blue from the sky, such that the dream becomes something we have lived. The dream is made of the stuff you cannot create and cannot kill, the stuff of the universe, inside us."

Polonius lay down on his back and looked up at the mirrors of smoke. His eyes seemed to see something up there that he loved and feared at once, the gory birth of a beautiful girl.

"November," he said.

"Polonius."

"Do you think it matters what we do?"

"I don't know. I think somewhere in that question

there is a wrong question, because there is no difference between me saying that everything matters, and nothing matters. Matters is the wrong word, Polonius. Who is going to come out and tell you that your thoughts are important, that they see the flares shooting flame, that they see you on fire? If the Lord God himself told you that he saw you, that you were shooting flames and on fire, would you listen? Would something change? I don't think so. I think there are thoughts that hem in, thoughts that contain us, and thoughts that expand, thoughts that pry us open. Actions too. The essence of freedom is to be able to choose, sometimes, between these types. I will sleep and dream, or I will wake and act, in every possible sense, in senses even unimaginable to us right now. I think I would be denigrating the thing if I tried to guess at where it comes from. It is an acrobatic act we need to practice, for sure."

This reminds me of a passage from *The World Meter*, which I must have inspired:

Not the freedom of the philistine with his pasteboard sign. Actual freedom has nothing to do with quantifiable freedom. Actual freedom is a sensation of the soul. What species of beggar is the "ruler" of your village has no bearing on the feast or famine that happens inside. Nor does the loosening of restraints, the casting of the body and mind into a pool where they may swim towards any horizon. Actual freedom can hate or love the restraints; it can seek or spurn solitude or company; it can refuse to visit some who have sought it actively all their lives; it can dwell in the hearts of others who have no name for it. You could call it a blessing, you could call it a form of madness.

We both lay down on the floor and stretched our bodies into taut breathing ribbons. Then we disappeared back into the dream.

—

NINE

"HARMONY AND HARMONICS"

Harmony and harmonics were the gods Federico worshipped, and he had perpetual shrines to them, guitars in the one corner, girls in the other, in his bedroom—a cavernous guest suite on the second floor of the house with a gauzy white carpet and a baronial wall of windows that made you feel that outside there should be birches and spindly pines and lakes and technicolor topless Germans. The shrines would migrate, the odd girl would pick up the odd guitar, but they generally kept to their corners. On the morning I am thinking about, the girl was Elise. During or after the night with the Chinese violinists, Elise had taken to him. She appreciated Rico's musical mastery, his sartorial sophistication, and his facility with Spanish and Portuguese and Italian. She appreciated his knowledge of books, his actual knowledge of books, his memory of whole passages. Elise, I could tell from the way her dark eyes set on me, had an intensely precise mind, the mind of an engineer mixed with the artistry of a conductress—very rare. On this particular morning Federico picked away on the guitar a classical tune by a Brazilian whose name I could never remember. Elise was drawing curves and arrows and symbols in a notebook, and twirling a ruby encrusted ring in her fingers.

I stood in the doorway. I asked Rico the same question I had asked November the preceding night, Does it matter at all what we do—or are we no more than straw men and women for the amusement of the gods, who are all either long dead or utterly mad?

Elise looked at me over her glasses. "Define what it means for something to matter," she said.

"We are asking the same question, I feel."

Federico lifted his eyes from his guitar and pulled his eyebrows up near his hairline, a sign of his vexation at being pulled out of his practice routine.

"Call it a matter of figure and ground," he said. "The nature of action, what is action? Do we act three times in our lives—when we are born, choose a mate, and die? Do we act a thousand million times, each time an image arises in our minds? Is it somewhere in the middle—every syllable, piss, shit, and fuck—or is that just instinct, is that just chaff? Hard to find figure and ground in that forest. So what now? It is all or nothing, it seems. Maybe that is as far as we are going to get. Everything or nothing. Everything is action, and everything matters, or nothing is action, and nothing matters. Anything in the middle leaves us with nothing but a quandary. You could spend your whole life wondering if you should have washed the dishes or not. The two poles are the only positions that can be taken at all."

"So you are either a philatelist or a nihilist," said Elise.

Rico's fingers glanced against the guitar strings, and he half-bent back into his practice, with his eyes looking back over his shoulder or up at the plasterwork of the ceiling as if the thoughts were going to come from over there or up there, which they often did. "And the philatelist may be the most ardent nihilist, and vice versa, because to have an opinion about such a thing, versus the vast humanity of imbeciles and bourgeoisie, who never really have an opinion about anything, is to cling stubbornly against the current to your rock of conviction. The monk and the soldier, no wonder they meet on the battlefield. Eh?"

"And which is which?" I said. "They both take extreme pains in their earthly routine in the name of the hereafter, which is again a mix of everything matters and nothing matters. The soldier cleans his rifle in a certain way, the priest cleans the chalice in a certain way—"

"And polishes the cock of the deacon in a certain way," said Elise.

"And the deacon polishes his cock back in a certain way, and the balls too, I'm sure, just as the soldier does the soldier. Both while chanting their canticles of chastity and orderliness and cleanliness. And the priest, while all this is going on, gives the soldier license to bring chaos raining down on women and children."

"Sex and blood, procreation and murder" said Elise. "What else is there in this world to let us know we are alive?"

Elise peered down at the ring she was twirling in her fingers. Federico began to speak through his guitar, I do not know the terms to describe his phrasing, it was as if he were praying to God to ask Him why He did not exist, and praying to the gods to ask them why they had gone unworshipped these thousands of years. Why should a god need to be worshipped? November's hand floated up behind me and pressed against my back, it sent shivers through my body as if pushing me out the end of a tunnel where I had lived in darkness—this is how her hand still feels.

"There remains art," I said.

"What are the themes of art?" said November.

From *The World Meter*:

I do not believe that we have done something, if we have not done it to the hilt. We are trying to do the something, sure, we are studying the something, but we have not done it. Yet how do we know when the something ends and the next thing begins, such that just before that point lies the "hilt"? You are running, running. How do you know you have run your fastest? Is it just before you reach the bus you are trying desperately to catch? Is it when you have out-run those three white barking dogs of your dreams? Is it when your feet lift off the ground and you fly?

TEN

"LET US REMEMBER"

Let us remember that we are bottomless. We are locked in time, intombed in time, so we imagine, for to fly off the wheel of these rounds would be to expose our lips to the pumice winds of immortality. To break the silence of this script, a set of stage directions without words, would be to cast ourselves into the purple night of the moonless sea. We pace a glass walled balcony, plied with drink on the outer reaches, and the sea speaks to us. What does she say?

It was, as I put it before, a grey and literary morning. All the clocks in the house could be heard measuring out the moments. Nobody drove by in the street. We were strung out, hollowed out of mind, body, and spirit, always hungry and never knowing why. The four of us had passed midterms of our senior year and were reading for our final theses—I had marked up the three volumes of Dante copiously with lines and pictures and faces, but had put nothing to paper of my own. Polonius had done the same to his volumes of *Either / Or*, and Rico, I think, did it to his entire library and ours. Polonius had shelved *The World Meter* and would not take it up again before our visits to Vermont that summer. Elise was trying to solve theorems, or something, on a pile of notepads, while Rico sat by smoking and marking up his markup of *The First Circle* and playing his guitar and feeding her wine. The wine! Our daily sustenance was two bottles of wine apiece, our teeth were stained royal purple. The cellar, as it had been left by my grandfather and barely depleted by Alexandra and her opera buddies, who only seemed to drink champagne, was always full no matter how thirsty we were, and the feeling of pulling a fresh bottle out of its cylinder never lost the excitement of knowing that we were going to be drunk in only a matter of time. We were ecstatic on the booze, our minds were blown yet ever ripe to be blown again.

It was not early in the morning but not late either. Call it 9.55, that is one of those times when, if you have been up for a while, you are ready to go back to bed—and this is how we felt, especially with the long unknown of composition looming over us, and our unwillingness to have it over with and emerge into a world that had no apparent means of embracing us. It was early Spring, the air outside was still thin and cool, eddies of draft slinked through the leaden windows and clawed at our ankles. Federico's fresh cigarette smoke was heavy and druggish and made vine lines and curlicues over his head.

"Sex and blood, procreation and murder," said Elise.

I had been standing in the hall pressing my bare feet against the grain of the ivory carpet that was cut close and dense so that you could turn it from ivory to blue shadow and back again with a sweep of the toe. My hands were playing with one another through the pockets of my cotton smock, my fingers groped across the fabric divide and walked back and forth across the seams of my hips and pelvis, smoothed down the fabric and smoothed tight the skin. I wanted to reach out to Polonius and touch him. I took my hands from my pockets and looked at them. The white light that seeped into the hall from the gallery of windows facing the garden showed my hands as translucent river deltas of green blue blood. What if I peeled the skin off my hands and saw the inner workings for myself? The alien glow of my blood, I thought, would not hold up, the blood would oxidize and show thick red, the sort that glazed me when I reached inside the ribcage of my first kill and cut the buck's heart from its perch. I threw it to the buzzards, and they majestically swirled down, the messengers of the underworld, and transformed the buck into a bird. I remembered looking at my hands that were shiny in the twilight with gore and thinking, I have just gained a new emotion. I pressed my hand against Polonius' back and felt him shiver under my touch as if electrified.

"There is art," said Polonius.

"What are the themes of art?" I said.

Rico was playing a midnight carnival by Tom Jobim. His fingers were moving so fast they were ghosts of themselves. Statement and retraction. Statement and restatement. Reaching out and doubling back. Sometimes the notes were like raindrops, other times they were like birdshot. Then they slowed down and walked in the rain and birdshot, sheltered by glossy armored raincoats. Rico smiled and he grimaced, he made faces you could not describe. Polonius and I, my hand still resting on his forgiving spine, were still with aural rapture. An incredible amount of time went by wherein none of us had any thoughts. Elise was drawing circles and squares in her notebook. Her toe twitched, but only because my eyesight was so still that it twitched when it focused on her perfectly still toe. My fingers moved between two of Polonius' vertebrae. They felt in the soft meat of his spine. I felt his life force vibrate and breathe under my fingers like the oscillations of a star.

The role of intoxication in the life of the mind has barely been treated, we slap a diagnosis on the subject and walk away. The fact of the intoxication of a great thinker is seen as counterpoint to his stature, an inexplicable lacuna in his character: he was a genius, but alas a drunk. No one says: he was a genius, and he never would have known it if he had not been blown out of his own mind a great deal—but we should say it thus more often. In order to do something new, something original, we need to see our own madness as something to be embraced. We need a phase shift. What is madness? I do not think it can be explained away, it must be demonstrated.

This is a long way of saying, that someone brought out the wine. Who brought out the wine? It could not have been Federico, he was still making music, his fingers were still ghosts. It could not have been I, for I stood and stared at Elise playing with her pubic hair under a pair of boxer shorts whose crotch was not wide enough for her modesty. Like Rose, Elise was a tiny girl with an expressive flourish of pink flesh between her legs, and unlike Rose, she left wild a fabulous tuft of dusky hair to crown that jewel. It was so gratifying for my fingertips to get through that gauzy tangle and reach the special skin that was softer and more weightless for the contrast. So it could not have been Elise either who fetched the wine, but I have the sense that I never let go of Polonius. Who else was there?

Someone brought out the wine and the magic powder, and before long it was night, and we were in the car. Polonius was driving with a bottle between his legs. He was driving like a man possessed by faith, we were going so fast that the faces of the buildings and people disappeared so ineluctably that they seemed to be getting flushed down into Hell behind us, and the eyes of the pedestrians were frozen into my mind as shocked fireflies emerging from hydroquinone into the scarlet dark room of the city. The howl of the engine rattled against the facades and wrestled with its own shadow over the rooftops. Then more speed, more drunkenness, more cokedness. The landscape had the yips, it tore the skin from its own face. The face of Philadelphia was swallowed up in the Schuylkill, in whose face gleamed Philadelphia. I reached my mind's hand out and scraped the surface of the river, I took a monstrous bump from my alpine fingernail, my mind was wet with blood. Polonius was screaming with joy. Rico had his guitar over his lap and Elise's, and their proximity spoke of the inimitable form of lust, their faces were joined at the tongue as he played. His fingers were going like silent terrors over the strings that spoke with a thousand voices without being touched. Spanish now, no Brazilian finery, Spanish dark and not clean, the song told of an army of widows that subdued a whole arena of bulls with their bare hands, the streets of Seville were Niles of black blood. Then they went to the cemetery and exhumed their dead husbands, spindly toreadors in green silks and gold plated cuirasses, and made love to the corpses. Emotionless midgets in charro suits with twirling feet danced and rapped their canes and chanted their approbation around the orgies. A plague of rabbits emerged from the opened graves and nibbled everything back to death and the whole dance started again. Flamenco. The trees, giant pines, got up on tiptoes and crept away from us, longlipped and devious, climbed the hill of the winding road we were ascending, lined the inner surface of the horizon and formed a dark huddle off in the distance across a field. Polonius turned off the road and followed them. He took a track that hid us from the road and civilization among tall stalks of wheat illumined by the moon that shone through a prismatic halo of clouds. I reached my hand out the window and let my palm ride the tips of the stalks as we cascaded over gentle waves of earth, a miniature mountain range of so many secret places. The crickets were screaming and jumping into the car. Federico played at his most furious, his hand spanned the neck of the guitar in ten or twelve arachnid flourishes. The Nile of blood spilled into the Mediterranean. We were released from the wheat field into a tufted grassland painted with the moon shadow of the giant pine trees, and all was still.

We got out of the car and looked around us. From where we stood we could not see the edges of the field, the curvature of the earth hid them from us. There were lights in the sky, signs of the city, but they were faint, as if from another planet. The air smelled and tasted of wet earth, and it moved as if possessed by an animal spirit, just as it had in the microclimates of the Clarion of my youth. Around us and above us were the huddled black pines, their tops occluded by their incredible heights. Each branch was talking to the branch across from it, saying, bless you, bless you: the space in their midst was a cathedral. The four of us, each alone, spread out in the nave of this vaulted understory, and we walked deep into its heart, into the shrines and the crypts and the haunted alcoves. No one had any words, we communicated by touching each other's hands and mouths and bodies. Elise came up to me and fell into my arms exhausted, we lay down on a bed of dirt and watched as Rico started climbing one of the giant trees, and Polonius not far behind him. They became squirrels, birds, they climbed up ten stories and disappeared. I nested in Elise's armpit and welcomed a surge of ecstatic paralysis. Elise shot me through with her warmth and it formed a quilt around my body, it touched the soles of my feet and wove itself through the hairs on my head. We could hear the boys hooting from the treetop, and their voices showered over us and made an igloo of peace in our midst. I rubbed Elise's stomach. She was soft, not like me, I was taut everywhere, her flesh was as buoyant as whipped cream. I reached around us for a bottle and took a swill, my god it felt good, and I tipped it into her mouth and she gulped again and again, and the tendrils of wine stained her cheeks and her hair which was fine as spider silk. We entered a mutual dream. Do you know what this is? It is a place where you are so fucked up that you communicate with yourself through the cosmos. The cosmos are a game of fingertips, sea bottoms, little sounds like the clicking of the tongue against the roof of the mouth, eyelashes against the smooth skin of the flank, the cosmos are the feeling that everything can be completely right and completely wrong at the same time, two poles that give equivalent feelings of pleasure: my mouth and Elise's ears, or her mouth and my ears, or I don't know and I don't know: the cosmos. Everything that ever happened moved through us at that moment, all in one go, and not on purpose or because we wanted it to but exactly because we had no purpose and we had no idea of wants, only fulfillments, at that moment. Yes, we were monstrously and even tumultuously fucked up, the world was constantly careening up to meet us, pouring us out and filling us up at the same time, tipping us over and catching us as it tumbled us about. Another swig, another guzzle, war whoops and celebrations from the trees, the boys were coming down, they had caught something, they had killed something.

The boys descended carrying a part of the tree, the very top, the torch, the trophy. They were black with sap and delirious. We rose, Elise and I, and we brought out more wine, more powder, more everything. More everything. We got plastered to the earth and the sky at once, and in between those poles there swarmed an incredible peace and clarity of mind, we looked at each other and saw each other's faces as if in technicolor for the first time. The treetop, planted in the dirt, stood so still that it shuddered in my gaze that was wavering. It desiccated, froze, dropped its needles by the exploding handful. We joined arms and bodies and huddled around watching it die.

The feeling at first took the guise of sadness. Millenia of the gods' creation were coming to an end, the gods whose loving fingers fashioned the elements and beckoned this one closer to that one, bid them marry and parse once more, set the gravitation of their relations to one another. You sea will claw away at the land and aspire to the skies. You sunlight will grace and curse the gardens and the deserts, and will find your way into forested hallways where small things will reach for you, let them believe that their quest is noble, that they can see you and touch you and not be alone. You terra will grow and divide into fine archipelagos and fold and writhe at your borders and break and pinch off in operatic headlands. You skies will invest the land with rippling mirrors in which your stars and moon may be multiplied, and your crystalline tears will coagulate and flow and form landscapes of their own, cradles in which the river and stream will feel safe. What happened then? As the Latin poet put it, creation was subjected to the appetites of creation. We, meaning all things animate and inanimate, found that we had a taste for each other. Lion for lamb and lion for lion. Storm for mountainside and storm for sea. Does not thunder over the ocean mimic the impassioned cry of a lover at the moment of climax? The feeling at the lip of a pit mine in the deserts of Atacama is one of relief, of awe that such a thing is possible, of pain for the loss of ground, of pleasure for the feeling of massive penetration. There is the appetite for nitrogen, hydrogen, oxygen, light, and silence marked by birdcalls. And there is the appetite to consume and be consumed. The passions of sex and suffering and infliction and affliction, they all got going at once. There were waves of acceptance, of giving in to the passions— golden ages when life and death and art flourished—and there were waves of restraint— dark ages when nothing flourished—and often these waves happened at the same time in different places, such that two swells would break on different beaches in isolation, or they would collide, making war, making purgatory. Virgins were defiled in the name of Diana.

Virgins were burned in the name of Jesus Christ. All sorts of unspeakable things happened to non-Virgins. Their hymens were sewn back again, their clitorises severed. Assholes were widened in the name of celibacy. Soldiers became monks, and altarboys became highwaymen. Art became pornography, pornography became art. The gods rested, but they could not sleep. They were confounded yet fascinated by their creation, and consumed by something that was not quite regret, not quite elation, a sadness.

The gods' sadness was ours at first, but only for a moment. We circled the treetop chanting unintelligibles, and we blew our minds out with intoxication, the sadness was peeled away like the darkness from the dawn. I remember I was holding the hands of Elise and Polonius, and I could not feel either of them, I squeezed as hard as I could but could not feel anything physical, I tried to feel the bounds of my skull but for all I knew they could not be described, my mind was a mandorla stretched between the earth and the heavens. The treetop burned, it went to ash, it disappeared, and I closed my eyes and opened them again, it grew and went to flame and ash and disappeared, and I closed my eyes and opened them again. Down in the base of my body, the cliffsides were melted and reconstituted as oceans of plasma, and I myself began to flow—into and out of place and around and around the circle of those arms that embraced me fully and unconditionally, and back and forth from my earliest childhood to my death. I was a pendulum that swung and swirled and made figure eights through time and space, my eyes began to see—they began to see all.

The most ancient report of those who claim to have been drugged into all-sightedness is that the universe is composed of gatherings of energy. The lightning bolt of Jove imbues the earth with heavenly energy, the forces of mysterious gravities act upon us, and the task is to tune our souls to receive those forces. Those who do receive at the highest levels are called enlightened, the shamans, the yogis, the high priests and prophets. Almost universally, the way to receive the message from above is to sit still—perhaps with some small rocking motion to stimulate the blood flow—and the message comes—it is some fantastic, garbled gibberish. It is confusion. The shaman must withdraw from the world, his mind is so full of heavenly static. He sees and hears too much. After a time he walks always with his head down, he is downright useless to the world. He tends to his rocky soil, his apple trees, his petrified soul. His sex is rendered neuter . . . . Now, just under the shamans, less refined and more open to earthly chaos, are the artists, the musicians, the poets, who let the thunderbolt arc from their spirits to their bodies. Their spines are electrified, their eyes, their nipples, their sex parts are all a-quiver. And so the spirit-current flows down the line until it reaches the unknowing child in the form of a carpet shock.

The ancients saw and felt the universe as pervasive energy, but I, spinning in that circle made of the delight and affection of my closest lovers, saw everything differently, I saw it in terms of origins. There is the sun, and there is the moon: the sun makes its own light, the moon receives and reflects. When I looked down at the Earth from my swinging heights, I saw the human race as a vast landscape of the spirit covered with a sort of lunar sea, with what looked from a distance like no more than twenty or thirty little torches casting their light on the surface of that moving mirror. The lights shimmered, each to each. Where were those torches? Who were they—or What were they? I roamed a dream landscape of my own making, inside my mind that knew what it had created and why, yet I could not understand what I myself had done.

After a while spinning and oscillating in space, I was captured by the Earth's gravity, and I began to fall. I fell towards something like the river Nile, let us call it the river Nile. The Nile was black as ice and infinitely deep, when I struck the water I barely made it back to the surface without suffocating. Above me were toy bridges suspended in the sky. I looked around, there was no one, then I opened my eyes.

Everyone was still moving, dancing, laughing, drinking, and my fingers were glistening with powder. We were still in the circle we had made for ourselves, the treetop was stuck in the ground, robust and deep green as ever. Someone had lit a fire, and our shadows made ghosts on the nightscape. I looked around me, I touched Federico, I touched Elise, I touched Polonius, they touched me, they took me in their arms, I still feel the embraces they gave me, the truth of the embraces, they told me, you will remember this moment as the point where you passed into nowhere, the point after which only one thing matters, and that thing is . . .

ELEVEN

"WHAT WE WANT IS TO LIVE"

What we want is to live with a sense of our direction. I do not know if the actual direction matters so much as our knowledge of it and our ability to reach a harmony with the implications. Nor do I know if the actual destination of our lives matters or even exists. As I wrote in *The World Meter*:

You cannot see, in life, where you are going until after you have reached there, and upon death there is no "afterwards". Thus it should hold that the end of our journey is never known to us—only the middle, and something of the beginning. When you connect the dots between your beginning and your middle and extrapolate with whatever organ you prefer to extrapolate with, you begin to understand your trajectory. There are infinite trajectories, just as there are infinite ways to draw a circle around a sphere. But there is only one for you, and after you begin to feel what it is, you will begin to know joy—even if you are headed for hellfire and damnation . . .

That night around the treetop when we all messed ourselves up beyond reckoning, November realized that she was headed for deliverance from all the world's waste and damnation. She realized that she was among the pearly torches she saw sugaring the sky. And the quality of her light was so pure that it cast even the most preposterous of history's villains as hiccoughs in the consciousness of the universal artist, who, having been awake for millions of millennia, sometimes dozed off on the magic carpet on the floor of her studio—and while she was dreaming of fields of rapeseed and lavender shaped by the winds into ocean swells, the pendulum of time struck at her sides and extracted bitter tears for the innocent. These were the tears that poured out of all of us, as we watched the crest of that giant pine take on the mantle of death.

Federico preserved the tree-trophy in the back seat of his Mirage. He brought it food and water and gave it his form of gymnospermal companionship, and it emerged out the roof of the car and became a giant again, it rained down its resinous seed pods on the city and our lives within the city. When in states of feeling inexplicable to all but ourselves, we—I, November, Federico, and Elise—would give a look to each other that signified somehow that pine and the experience of that night in the field, the nameless field that we would never find again, and we would understand that the space defined by us four sitting or waiting in line or lying on top of one another as the case may be, we would understand that that space represented a blue hole in the human cosmos, the velvet reflection of a sunset only we could see.

We went on to take doctorates. Federico in Music, I in History, November in Drama and Desdemona, and Elise in Engineering. We all stayed at Pennsylvania—there was no question of leaving the economic wastes and intellectual splendor of Philadelphia—and we spent those years as fucked up as we could achieve without killing ourselves. My dissertation advisor tried to expel me on several occasions, but he could not—I delivered pages scattered with impossible and often inscrutable styles of English language yet expressing ideas so rare in their originality that each time Conway registered his complaint, his mouth would stop itself, he would hike up his one pant leg revealing a shocking argyle, light a cigarette, and burn a hole through his own protest.

Professor Dennis Conway was a tremendously well-respected eccentric historian of Medieval France and Russia and Japan and ancient Greece and Rome and Byzantium. He had spent his whole life in libraries. His skin was so white and so thin and so brittle that the man could be heard to crepitate as he walked the halls of the College. I believe he still had a wife, for his clothing was impeccable and impeccably pressed. In his offices he would smoke to his heart's content, for at this point his heart could not beat without the smoke. As the cylinder between his fingers would start to burn down—a long cylinder it always was—and gather ash, he would flick off the ash and stub out the swan's neck of a cigarette in a mass grave of an ashtray full of disfigured and dismembered bodies of cigarettes past, and then he would light another. It had to be fresh, for some reason, fresh smoke. He had a special ventilator that kept the smoke in the room moving. Therefore his incredible shelves of notes and notebooks, Latin and Greek and Persian volumes and commentaries on commentaries, would wave like fan corals on a polluted reef. He had a marble bust of Pope Joan on a Corinthian pedestal, even she looked to have aged badly. There was a capacious balcony adjacent to Conway's offices, but Conway had no use for it. The windows were furry with the pollen of the years, for Conway was very old, so old that his arms had shrunken in past the cuffs of his shirtsleeves—he had to roll the sleeves up, and in the roll would be a handkerchief, and in that handkerchief the snot from so many public nose blowings.

The sign on Conway's door read in Latin, "Respect Your Local Medievalist", and then in French, "History is For The Dead". The rug on the floor was from Istanbul, it was elegantly frayed and rat-eaten and stained with opium tar. The design in the rug—I want to say it was a whole lot of trumpets intertwined with ficus and fruits, pomegranates, fruits of the Medici. Like all Medievalists, Conway was quite taken with the Medici. He would call them all by their first names—Cosimo and Lorenzo and Giovanni—and each name had its own flavor. For instance, Cosimo had the flavor of a beloved child. Lorenzo—il magnifico—had the flavor of a virtuosic goalkeeper. And Giovanni had the flavor of a man who worked at the local pizza parlor. Giovanni was a lament. Conway was a knower and lover of all things beautiful, therefore he often spoke to himself in Catalan, and I remember him in a Catalan accent, whispering through his nose, as it were, while he smoked, the word *Giovanni*.

Conway wrote in orthodox scholarly fashion, his sentences no more than prompts for his eloquent and prodigious footnotes. If he did employ humor, it was with the restraint of the Swiss. *The Huns were, if not utterly misunderstood by the Romans, the Greeks, the Gauls, and modern historians, then at least half.* Conway had placed more than six hundred seventy-five publications in esoteric journals, and he made sure that his visitors sat under the shelf that sagged under the weight of those six hundred seventy-five reprints, as if to utter a stray word would cause the dry tonnage of all Conway's intellectual output to drop like a guillotine.

I have an image of Conway defeated, flummoxed, blown away, his upper spine collapsed over the draft of my dissertation. He had run out of adjectives and metaphors to describe how objectionable he found my prose, so he was simply reading aloud. *The currents between Indefatigable and Isla Morosa may have been flowing in reverse that day, hence the nauseated crew—or it was the pescado, which was getting rough in the hold, the brand of Salonican sea salt used by the Beagle being slimy and easily dissuaded from the sides of the fish.*

"Are you trying to see if my own writing will offend me, Professor Conway? I do not think that writing has the ability to offend its writer, it would be as if I were offended by the smell of my own ordure."

"I'm not trying to offend you, Mr. O'Mara." Conway lit a cigarette, took a drag, stamped it out, and lit another. "I just started crossing out pages, I just can't go through the exercise of reading all these *words*. You need to stop using so many words."

"Professor Conway, with respect, I need to use words, I don't have a choice. The god damn thing needs to be two hundred pages long."

"But you do have a choice . . . " (Stamp, stamp, fire, puff, the smoke was a pregnant raincloud over my head). "You do have a choice. There are words and there are words. For example. Let me see. Let me see."

Conway paged through the manuscript, and it took a while, for he took many smoke breaks, during which I observed that paging through something must require two hands, though I could not make out what the non-paging hand was really good for.

"*The oracular and apparitional glower of the tortoise, which to cant requires the telescope of its maliferous neck, turning the animal into a cartoon version of an emaciated snail—the eye of the tortoise smote the cormorants—they were afraid to fly, lest the tortoise become a ghastly giraffe and pluck them from the skies as they launched and shat.* How do I place this sentence in the context of history—this idle and fantastical, indeed cartoonish description of something you have never seen, not to mention the implication of causation where there very well may be none. Why not simply say, *There were tortoises, whose description the reader may reference in Voyage of the Beagle 2:141. And there were flightless cormorants,* and footnote Beebe perhaps. Include the description in a footnote. But you shun footnotes, to my great chagrin. The reader of a history is interested in fact. You have not a single actual fact in this entire work."

During this brief soliloquy, the nearly bald Conway had smoked the tips of an entire pack of cigarettes. He opened another. I could now barely see him through the sullied air. It did not help that Conway did not get outdoors much: he smelled like an abandoned codfish. I let him talk for the good part of an hour more, and I trawled my gaze away from his crumpled face and over his stacks of flamboyantly bound books—the complete works of Darwin, the complete works of Lao Tse, the complete works of Chaucer, the complete works of Flaubert. I still remember the daydream I had sitting in that seat, that unseasonably hot day in April, we were both sweating, sweat dripped from Conway's smoking hand and stained his cuff purple—sitting in that seat and being told that my writing was garbage. I dreamed of Brighton Beach, of the earthshattering scream of the elevated trains, of the bodies of Anna Delancey, the live body and the dead body, the body in its young perfection, the body in its full and taut past, and then the mark it left when it vanished out of sight and permanently into my mind. The figure of Anna Delancey was branded on the walls of the sanctum sanctorum of my brain, I dreamed of her as if I were about to see her that very evening. When she became suddenly aroused, especially when awakened in the wee hours of morning, in her mouth I could taste the simmering heart of her pelvis, her sex stretched out in the sun to steam and rot, the ripe cantaloupe of her fertility. Anna Delancey waited for me under the train tracks in her torn shorts, the pockets protruding from under the frayed hems, and a shroud of a tank top that made her look more than naked, her tiny nipples visibly triumphant. In her hands, cradled like a dear child, was a forbidden book in a foreign tongue printed on newsprint and wrapped in rice paper. Cerebyani Golub—*The Silver Dove*. Three of her fingers bore the silver-plated rings I had given her over the years, they were tarnished like spoiled mirrors, but they leant *The Silver Dove* a biblical air, as if Anna were about to preach from the centerline of Brighton Avenue to the pensioners in the doorways. The mist of the ocean behind her, too, shone silver over its background of dove blue, and steady piano notes of sunlight alternated with the shades cast by twelve or twenty puffy floaters, and gave life to the shades of the buildings. An old woman lingered on the curb and waited for the light to turn, her shopping cart full of old *Pravdas*. Anna and I collided, and as we stood there locked in cupola I felt her spirit clamor against her tiny ribcage. We walked to the beach and lay down on the sand and I felt her weight on me for hours and hours until long after the sun went down. Our eyes were squeezed shut against the world. Every voice we heard against the crashing of the waves was like the first voice. Then—as happens in dreams—I awoke under Anna Delancey in the library, and my face was wet with her tears. Our bodies washed down the Schuylkill and were caught in the ocean's gyre, we rolled in the undercurrents and were swallowed up into Hell.

Conway was still talking and smoking. He was nearing the point of having pushed a zeppelin of smoke out the ventilator.

"... I know this is incredibly burdensome, and you do not want to heed my warnings, but you are not a scholar, Mr. O'Mara, you are something else. And that something else, I don't know what it is, it may be some kind of artist, a poet. Everyone hates poets, but a poet you may be. God help you."

Down in Hell, there was an amphitheater, just as Milton predicted. It was hot, but nothing was on fire. There were palm trees. It was a sort of tropical vacation for the spirit.

". . . So, Mr. O'Mara, you have twenty-four hours to re-write this dissertation, I will give you forty-eight. You need to find something concrete to say, or I will have to fail you."

I thanked Conway for his time, and took my leave of him. To breathe the air in the hallway was like being in outer space.

Federico was wandering around looking for me. He was wearing a red bandana around his neck. His face was gathered around his nose from drugs and monstrous gouts of sleeplessness and self-inflicted starvation and overindulgence in delirium.

"So, what's the verdict," he said after about a half mile of walking. We were going home, to November and Elise. I did not answer him, I just looked at him. I was so satisfied with my place in obscurity, so content with my limitless freedom, that I had no need of words.

TWELVE

"ELISE WAS PROPPED UP"

Elise was propped up on her pillow. She stuck her fingers inside herself and took them out and licked them and drew little Catalan mustachios of blood on either side of her face.

"You know something?" she said.

"What," I said.

"You never know who you are, and you never know who other people are, until it's too late." She took another dip with her fingers. Her crotch looked like a very desultory cubist version of the Battle of the Bulge painted onto an immaculate pussy.

"You could say, we never know anything before it's too late."

"Because knowing implies that something is complete, that it is finished. That the canvas is about to be framed and hung in the parlor, and it will become history, as concrete as a headstone, and just as irrevocable."

She drew a bloody mouth around her mouth, and she painted her lips blood red. She beckoned me to kiss her. I did. She tasted like the molten stuff at the center of the Earth. I let her mark my nipples, and when I looked in the mirror they appeared as the two livid eyes of the Sun. I encapsulated that image in my theatre dress, a pair of body tights and the corset I would wear when Othello killed me, again.

"What is it that you know, Elise, that cannot be taken back?"

She painted little devil's horns on her forehead, that made her look like a massacred billy-goat. "I have no idea, I just feel it coming, like the rain." She bounced off the bed and into the bathroom, and she left a trail on the rug of mismatched spots that took their place as poisonous fruits on a pattern of what could have been quaking columns of bay leaves, but also might have been the silhouette of the ornate iron gates that guarded the imagined garden beyond. I finished tying myself up—the hair and the belt and the strings of the corset and the thick leather boots, and I looked in on Elise as she showered against stark white glass tile. The blood ran in a continuous stream down her leg and into a red Nile of ambitious rivulets and lazy serpentine routes. Whipping-post droplets collected on the walls in a way that no other substance can collect. Nature must have had such a towering moral sense, I thought, to have sown such a permanent marker of our mortality inside of us. Or (I thought too), Nature was a relentless tease and a straightjacket mad murderess, what with the plainness she painted on our skin and the monthly signs she gave us of the gory universe within.

I stood in the doorway watching Elise. She was pushing thirty, but her nipples still supplicated the heavens. Her skin was so taut and perfect, like a dust jacket wrapped around her flesh. She had but two dimples on her body, on either corner of her buttocks. Her toes spread like flower petals when she touched them. She was so petite I could hold her in one palm. In the white tile wall of the shower I felt that I could see the shine of her eyes. Desire cloyed and got under my corset and under my skin, my whole body began to itch as if I had waded in poison ivy, bathed in paper cuts. Downstairs, the powder room mirror showed trouble— my face was covered in spots, yellow and brown and pink like a face buried in sand—by god it was only my face, but all I saw was a shattered face. A car was waiting outside, Federico.

It was Federico only, in the car. Polonius was gone, and I was free. Philadelphia and her boys and girls were at the peak of their gritty bloom. The air was alive as if rushing to fuel the fire of some tremendous orgy on Olympus, and that breeze was always tickling the tiny hairs on my arms and buffeting the labyrinth between my legs and making it quake.

How many were there that summer? Until that particular night of Othello, the twelfth or twentieth night of an infinite run of Othellos, there were many, each of them shrouded in different shades and textures of hot darkness. But the number of my lovers was not my pleasure so much as the feeling that I was always shifting, always changing, like the sea, around the people I did in fact love. I became so obsessed with Federico and Elise that I would moan for them in every exhalation, I would fiend for them as one fiends for a drug, even when they were in my arms. They were my faithful, I was their slave, I was their faithful, they were my slaves, we lived nested to infinity inside of one another. And the most fearful part, we did not (we still do not) fear that one or another of us would ever depart the circle. In our blood bond that was stronger than blood, we saw our own deaths and dreams reflected. We roamed together on the rooftops of the world. Purple fulminous skies. Peace. Our hands and bodies intertwined, waiting for the dawn, waiting for Polonius. Desperate for another slug of the lips that invades the veins and paralyzes all fear and doubt, pushes us beyond our deaths to a place where no one is born and no one ever perishes, an underground river whose black waters vanquish us and regurgitate us immortal. Holy intercourse.

Only Federico was in the car, and when I climbed in, I laid down and embraced his torso and let him cradle my head in his lap as he drove. He grew up painfully I am sure and despite himself against my cheek. Federico was touchy, meaning in his case that he did not like to be touched unless he was being touched to fruition. He took his hand off me. I swallowed him down. When we pulled into the garage under the theatre, my lips had gathered a new sheen as if I'd been dining on parmacetti. My eyes, too, had a waxy glow.

By this time I had chaired the Philadelphia Shakespeare Company for ten years, since my dissertation on the role of kingship in *King Lear* won the Lithecombe Prize. We rotated all the major works through on a five-year schedule but for Othello, whose murderousness was paraded forth every year for three weeks to a full house. Every other play I directed without casting myself, but I could not find a girl to play Desdemona: no one seemed able to wrap their minds around the dual fact that Desdemona does not deserve to die, though she opens her legs for the entire Venetian regiment. The play does not make Shakespearean sense otherwise—if Desdemona were merely innocent, then the bard wasted his breath on a cross-legged morality tale intended for no one, and the bard never wasted his breath. My casting calls were full of chalky, meek, prim and prudish girls from Radcliffe and pierced lesbian whores from Wesleyan. No one could play the role as well as I—I was the angel of assignation. My body—long, lithe, wisplike, arachnine—looked as if it could be batted about by a slight breeze like a smoke signal, but when it moved you could see that in the absence of apparent stores of energy, the thing moved by dint of its own sexual deviance. The I that walked the stage and the I that walked the sidewalks was never satisfied. I needed to know that my hands, when dispatched along the bare newborn skin along the hip joint of a man or woman, would make them renounce their homes, their families, their lovers—would make them die for just one more touch.

The car sat and caressed the ears over and over. It was a Bondy car, I forget the model, a hilariously Bondy car for such a humble man—Federico's finger pickings were playing on every crack radio in Rio De Janeiro, and even the most cultivated ponytailed little Latin girls would find themselves sweating all over him in the pissy bathrooms of Santiago. Federico—he was smaller than me, his ribs protruded like iron claws, you could not even pinch a pinch of snuff off his hollow frame, but he was a hero, a hero fucker, there were moments when his cock extended above his eyebrows, and when we had all given in and were beyond sleep, in a realm of ooze and hallucinatory conversations with people who could not possibly be there, he was still going, torturing us with pleasure—and now, in the meantime, he waited there in the running car for me like a cat, entirely still, watching the blood flow behind his own eyes. The red lights of the dashboard colored him. I wiped my lips to spread the pain of not seeing him again for three whole hours, or more.

The audience in its champagne stupor on those little velvet chairs is lucky. It has no idea how it feels to be on stage. In the darkness behind the curtain you are safe as a baby in the womb. In the bright lights you are an aborted embryo squirming in a jar. They call it acting, but in truth there is no place where one is more oneself than the stage. You are so hot, and time is moving like a palpitating heart, so you cannot think in forethoughts, you can only think with your body that leaves little echoes in your crux of what your body has said and done, illegible cuneiform scratchings on a moonlit cliffside that scare the hell out of you. You have fornicated with the entire Venetian regiment. You have lied. You are dead. There is a star on the horizon whose light bends into the room in defiance of perspective, becomes a fleeing portent of lashings to your heart. The echoes, like echoes under the sea, reveal very little about reality, just as the pebble grind of an engine in the ears of the diver is the same whether it belongs to a tanker or a dinghy, and the fleet of sailing ships passes soundlessly. On stage we are as without skin. Our intentions are stripped down to the musk of threatened survival, and our memories function only as memories of dreams. The actress is a living work of art.

To speak of dreams, I tend to catalogue the chapters of my life by their invisible ink, the worlds I lived in when I was asleep. I remember my youth as a certain landscape in black and white, with white lightning defining an enervated sky in the offing and sometimes trucking down to Earth and forcing me to seek shelter in sterile rectilinear brutalist postmodern spaces that spoke to the youth of my dream-architect. At the dawn of my adulthood, in my middle twenties you could say, the sun started to come out. Long grasses were, still are, bleached gold. Facades and woods stood out in technicolor. People were not so watery and nondescript, and their voices, if not always identifiable, would speak from some actual place in the landscape. Other sounds came alive, the far-off hum of a highway, or the yapping of a den of coyotes. The lightning of my former years was reduced to the glisten of dew on the reeds. The recurring scene of the baths of an emperor. All the men and girls in my life reclined in their niches like melted saints. Their skin was slippery with steam, and their faces told me that they knew me better than I knew myself—a terrible conundrum, for they were all inside me, and why did my mouths withhold from me

all my secrets? Always just beyond my reach—everything. The mysteries, say the gods, keep you dreaming.

When I left Federico watching the blood flow behind
his eyes in his Bondy car, what sort of dreams formed
the background to that scene? I had known loss—not so
great as Polonius' perhaps—not the drowning suicide of
his Anna and the wholesale loss of his childhood—but
my mother was gone—enough to set me dreaming of
resurrection, and waking up concussed by imaginary
tears. The Clarion farm was a setting, in so many metamorphosed forms. There was some sense of urgency, but
I never knew for what—something to run from, with no
sense of what it was or where it came from. My mother
was never dead in those dreams, she would be rocking
in a hammock on the terrace smoking, and say Johnno
or my father or the horse trainer Jacala would be dead
instead. Oblivious, my mother would drone on about
shades of stain for the library paneling, the fabric of a
cushion, the tastes of different jams, the cost of pound
cake. These were things she would never have deigned
to speak of when she was alive, and I would despair to
learn that her spirit, in the afterlife, was yearning for
the mundane trappings of earthly existence. The two
of us would hover there on the terrace like two idiots.
Around us, the landscape would reel, injected with an
hallucinatory drug. The feeling was of the pain of a sun
setting, and no wine to fuel the night. Dry.

I walked onstage. The lights came up. Why must it go this way, I said to myself when I felt the heat. Why can I not find another Desdemona in all the world. Why and why. No and No—then Yes and Yes.

So it is when we experience the fetish that is Tragedy, we ride on a highly electrified, razor thin rail of the soul. Our conscience tells us to leap off, yet our nature, magnetized and aroused, cries out for the feeling of cold steel against our spine.

THIRTEEN

"I STOOD IN A RIVER WITH COLLINE"

I stood in a river with Colline. The landscape flowed in place like the leaves of a palm around our nakedness. A hiker with nothing on but a backpack like a painted Indian craning over him for the view, must have been a German, stood some way off. I closed my eyes. Colline closed her eyes too, I would guess, because when I opened mine, hers were closed. Together we negated the existence of everything, then we drove back towards Los Angeles, where everything seems to exist despite everyone's best efforts. The relative cleanliness of the highways and streets, the crucible of Hell sanitized by flame. Mountains that could have been successive Mount Zions cut clean through by roads and power lines, like the sex parts of ravaged adolescent girls, and the skies gagged with rust. I must admit I didn't care about those particular mountains or skies—at that time I cared about Colline—I could speak to her. Colline was an artist who had moved beyond art. I was an historian who had moved beyond history. *The World Meter* had been printed in fourteen languages, was on its umpteenth edition, my writing had turned entirely inward and inscrutable, my tenure was indestructible, I was playing the part of the vertiginous Professor. I was also never not thinking about undressing someone, and my carrell at the Huntington smelled like the ladies' lounge at the theatre—lipstick, cigarettes, blood, and little rivulets of girlish air. A great deal of the reason for my towering libido—if things do have reasons, and I believe they do not—but then what do we say?—was that when I was away from November, I needed to replace her immediately. And November was not replaceable by one girl or three. It took an army, a collective spread over the vast fuck-state of California.

"What do you think it means Colline, this inhumanity around us, these horizons sullied with rectilinear forms, this sky shot through with napalm? The sun cannot even rise anymore."

"To me it speaks of a world that has discarded meaning, as a watch that fails to tell time. So we who embrace the ethereal owe nothing more to it. It is a curious sort of freedom, to know that nobody cares. It makes me want to—"

"It makes you want to what."

"I don't know—I don't know what I would want to do if things were otherwise. For now, and for the next one hundred years, I just want to fuck myself up and then unfuck myself in the morning. To leave and come back to the world, like a tide of constellations."

"And to leave and come back to me."

"Just not now."

"Not now."

"Not now."

"But you know I will. Or you will."

"Yes I know you will. Or I will."

"Because you and I will take many forms. And we ourselves are forms of what came before."

"And you cannot tell what form you will take next, or whose body this spirit will inhabit."

"Or why there is anything, or why anything becomes anything else."

"Why there is love, you mean."

"And what is it."

"And why is it so different from the love between me and my husband, or you and your . . . girl, or whatever you call her, or our other ones."

"And who can possibly get between us, but another you, and another me."

"Who can possibly."

"Another you. Is there another?"

"There are thousands, perhaps. Millions."

"All collapsed into your perfect form at this moment, only to collapse into a million forms, when you leave."

"If I were perfect you would not want me."

"Perfect as in complete, not as in China doll."

"Perfect as in I am yours."

"Perfect as in you are not mine."

She was curled up like a cartoon Sphynx, her legs had tied themselves in a Gordian knot, and the image of her skin against the asparagus piss flatulence of the Los Angeles air was like a pool of mercury poured into the open hand of a corpse—a pore in reality through which all my reservations and thoughts of abandoning her under pitiful circumstances and abandoning things generally could—temporarily—be scattered about the landscape and dispersed as so many wind-blown seeds. The strength of Colline's influence on me did not owe itself to beauty—she was fifty-three or five and had had three children, her body was a hieroglyph of the abuses of time. The hands especially were rough and papery from doing things. The skin behind her ears was accordioned from a facelift that had branded a slight sign of struggle into her smile. The stomach was overtaut too, like a clambake—and over the pudenda but just below the tanline there was that suture scar, not caeserian. The behind could be manipulated so as to appear entirely flat or a creamy rondure, it was delirious and disengaged, like a dilletante. When pieced together, these parts did vibrate in the right balance, and her eyes did glow like suggestions of moons behind hazes of clouds, and her teeth were perfect, and her skin shone bronze like the horseman—and she was an artist who had moved beyond art, as I said—but most of all she was married to another man. Otherwise—if she had not had a husband, and a good man at that—if her presence did not have the whiff of danger—if she had not been risking her life and livelihood, and something of mine, to be with me—I would not have been interested in her at all. I was then, as I am now, as I cannot but be, obsessed with the extremes. If I could not live at one or another—and there are more than two, there are as many extremes in life as there are in the universe—I would be dead. I had to be running, fucking, writing, or getting run over, fucked up, or written off. And when it came time to sleep—sleep is not a state of rest but a no man's land middle passage between ecstasy and despair, its own extreme of divided consciousness—the inside of my skin would itch, and I would writhe there until I woke up. Or else, when the gin actually hit the spot, I would lie in bed until morning feeling incredible, awake and not wanting to wake up. I wrote best in these middle night moments, when time did not harry me. I wrote about men and women and conceits that never existed and should not—about Biblical and

Homeric tumults of the soul that can only be read, for if they were experienced our hearts would pop in their cages from sentimental gluttony. Imagination, another extreme, an extreme of creation that is limitless, as if our minds were constantly expanding along the borderlines of the universe, imagination was my guide in all this—but I couched my books in language that made my imaginings sound like truth—hence Philosophy. The turn of phrase that conveys a sense of fact is so easy to pull off, it is almost nauseating. It goes something like this: And at this absurd hour I can only say *one* thing, that the *sole* thought on my mind is *death*, yet death *does not exist.* Say something that cannot be proven or disproven, but say it as if it is the only possible thing to say. We cannot know what is the sole thing on our minds, for our minds do not possess the capacity to tally up their contents. And how to think of death, when one does not know what it is—and how to know that an unknown exists or does not?

Colline closed her eyes again. It looked as if a Pharaoh's mask had been placed over her face. We reached Venice and tracked the ocean for a while and climbed out of the toilet bowl of the city and up into the Palisades. The air thinned, the colors came out. Someone's pandemonium of parakeets long escaped from their cage roosted in the magnolia in my yard, their conversation fell on us like fairy dust. The rest of this afternoon was going to be peace pierced only by the clamor of erotica, I was going to drown in Colline's eyes and drink up her kisses that tumbled me into aspen pitches—and after that I was going to expire—I could feel it. And after we passed the parakeets and Colline made a dinner of an Israeli cabbage soup that burned my palate and loosened my guts, we drank a liter of gin and did expire, interlocked.

I woke up in the middle of the night. She was gone, and I felt as if I'd been drowned and resuscitated in a place where the temperature just wasn't right. The lights were on, some candles were still burning in the halls and the great room. I walked outside naked. The parakeets were gone and the silence felt like it was flooding my head to swell beyond its borders. The silent silence, not the one described and circumscribed by the small beasts of the night, and the raw silence, for its backstop was the screech of cars along the One far below, sucked me into a vacuum of being, a continuous dry heave of the spirit. My usual phantoms—my November that I carried with me, my Elise that I carried, my Anna Delancey that I buoyed up on black rivers, my countless others, my dear Federico—had all flown. The fat hairy fucker remained. I wasn't really fat, I was bloated, and I was hairy as a porcupine. I felt inflated in a way I hadn't since the days the train trellises sheltered me by the slag heaps and rip-rap of the Schuylkill, and I would awaken in the middle of the night with my skin so taut my whole body was numb with the pain of impossible parturition. On those nights next to the river I would crawl on all fours to the bank and douse my head in the ravaged waters so thick with oil they would glow in the dark as if glutted with plankton. The cold shock of those miasmic waters would heighten the static in my mind, wear it out, and I would lie inside my blanket with my hand against Anna's porcelain bottom and compose my music. *The life of a philosopher is a farce of a farce—the backdoor of truth—a scorpion dream.* Porcelain and scorpion—when time slows down to a trickle, such feelings cross pollinate and bear delicate fruit.

Still naked, still hairy and still bloated, I went back inside. I sought out a fresh notebook and picked up my pencil, but something about the feel or shape of it didn't make sense to me. Each corner of the octagon felt inhumanely sharp, and when I placed the point of the pencil on the virgin surface of the page I felt that my mind was so full that it was too tight at the seams to let loose without causing massive hemorrhaging. And the inner material I could see through the mind's pores seemed to be written in a language I did not know. The characters were crooked and scrambled, as if reflected in an unfaithful mirror. When I looked more closely, a whiff of nausea overcame me, and the globe tilted precariously off its axis. What was I hiding from myself?

I drove down to the ocean. My hands shook, my orphaned cock retreated, my heart quaked in time with the motor of my Fiat. Although there was no one on the road, I felt on the verge of an horrendous collision. Everyone and everything was in danger, and history was turned on its head to reveal the evergreen hemorrhoids of human agony. I arrived at the spooked bluffs of Malibu, and I dug my feet into the rubbery sand. The ocean bore great plumes of horror, in the churn that numbed my feet I could feel the tickle of the feathers of death, yet I pushed on into the depths and found an oily calm beyond the break of the waves. I lay back and starfished myself on the surface, I caressed the thin film between the seen and unseen, between here and lost, and I could feel my body dim and reilluminate itself. The partitions between time and no time, between the known and unknown worlds, began to blur.

The canopy of stars viewed from the night sea without the intermediary of sail or ship is what I might call a connoisseur's view of the universe. One must have madness, or abandon—the ability to value something evanescent above something permanent. And one must have the ability to endure the unassailable fact that outer space is a physical representation of eternity—and between us and eternity there is nothing. I could feel that the undertow would not let me drift to safety without wearing myself out. My limbs numbed up into magic wands full of confetti. My heartbeat slipped into a stochastic whisper. Mind and soul, or numen you could say, remained. In a form not linear and not so much linguistic as revelatory, in the language of a razor against a multilayered canvas, the nothingness between here and space became what it was—a superfluous expression that could be nixed to zero, leaving me and eternity as Siamese twins separated at birth, staring at each other from opposite sides of an attenuated equals sign. I and I.

Polonius, said Polonius, who was no-one, you do not understand what equivalency means in the cosmic context. It does not mean what the rodents of logic are chittering about, in their cages, their playland fantasies. Mathematicians caked in snot and earwax. And your statesmen, lathered in bird droppings, quacking from psittacosis. Equivalency does not mean that one thing is or will ever become the other—or that they weigh the same on some sort of ultimate scale. There is no ultimate and there is no scale, things do not have beginnings and ends, and they do not have middles. It does not mean . . . It does not *mean.*

The statement naturally and immediately made me feel very cold, despite my numbness. It was nearly impossible to get back to shore, and I would have perished had the ocean not tipped over and dumped me out. I stripped naked and found my Fiat, which was still purring and had drifted in neutral to rest against a dune with its hind quarters up in the air as if it were a cat that had been pricked. The foredawn was suddenly apparent, like autumn, and the mountains went from steel to purple to flame in the course of my drive.

I had already written so many works that verged on the nihilistic (I thought, back on my couch and a shivering caterpillar in my blanket)—I had risked nihilism but I had stopped far short by retaining values in the form of feelings and wants. Love is no *thing* in and of itself, but your desire to make the thing you call love or to give it or to feel it—that indeed is something. Or so I had written. My other I, this cosmic I, wanted to negate even the idea that I could write about such things—for (and I hope you can follow me) if there is no such thing as one thing being another, words no longer trundle meanings.

I awoke very late the next day, and every day thereafter for the remainder of the summer. I awoke alone. I sent all my birds, black birds and white birds and water foul alike, skittering away. Colline was especially hurt, I did not care. So was Allison, I did not care. And Professor Emily Hughes, who had written my letter of reference to the Huntington—she was hurt too. I did not care. The article on Plato's *Symposium* versus Camus' *The Plague*—could fuck off. Bills and invoices, water and electric, credit cards, handymen, maids and handmaids, all fucked off. Callers, friends, visiting scholars, talks, dissertations, symposia, cocktails, recitals, prostitutish prudes, knightings, whale watchings, demonstrations, musicians, drug pushers, all fucked off. The time I spent immobile in a dream state, my gaze focused inward on the glassy surface of my mind. If there were no words— what was there?

My newfound sense, or was it fear, of infinite recursion arrested so many themes in my personality, froze them in amber like a breath never released. What I did not see at first, but felt as the nights gave into mornings and the days into soul wrenching evenings, was that holding my known life stationary allowed my unknown life to flourish. Imagine someone telling you, do not one thing tomorrow that you did today. The result was a form of confusion, a form of delirium and consciousness and even mind-soul integration, achieved at the expense of everything and everyone around me. Condensation of the argus eyed droplets of my inner matter and a sense of what you might call the essential momentum of existence.

It may have been days, it may have been years. The massive fig tree that enveloped my sleeping couch made itself a rusty shadow of leaves. The palm in the corner flourished inordinately, then it was dead and gone, then it was the beak of an egret. My belongings, once scattered in the bedsheets and boudoirs of my lovers, began to congregate on the front porch like old friends. In the middles of the nights, there came polite and then increasingly frantic knocks at the front door, and then silence, the foreboding crash of a car door, screams of defeat from inside the prism. After these screams died away, the silence materialized in me as a violent shiver of gratification. It gave me great solace to be alone, for only when I was alone could I admit to myself that I was living with the dead Anna Delancey.

The basis of religion and psychology is the aspirational notion that we can be delivered from suffering. But what is suffering, and what comes after? The religious answer runs: suffering is life, and deliverance comes only after death and through death. Your wandering spirit will return and haunt the man who stole your overcoat—in rage and glory. Psychology is more optimistic: suffering is your childhood, and deliverance may be lived out in an adulthood that is conscious of its roots but not utterly reliant on them. The transition may be achieved by watching reruns of your most horrifying memories until the nerves of your psyche have gone numb. In a paranoid lithium-induced coma you will then live out your days—in rage and glory.

Religion and psychology are not per se remiss in dreaming of a state of being in which one might live without pain. The problem is, sensation is a spectrum twisted into a gyre, such that no "left" or "right" exists—pain is born from and incubated in the womb of pleasure, love is a form of suffering, and suffering a form of love. One might say there is no one without the other—but in truth there is no "one" and "the other"— we are made of this stuff that flows freely within us, we are inextricably intermingled with ourselves—and with the others that we carry within ourselves.

That catatonic summer on top of the Palisades, brought on by what should have been a routine case of writer's block, I found Anna Delancey again. I found her in the world and within myself, and I followed her or she followed me everywhere—it was sometimes hard to figure out who followed whom. At times I would not be able to find her—or I would remark to myself that she was in fact dead—and I would fall into a ter- rific black hole, bespattered and choked with tears and lubricated with gin—at the bottom of which I would find her again. We had experiences that people cannot have—these I cannot describe. We revisited places of our youth in the exact state in which we left them, in the exact state in which they left us. We leafed through forbidden books that left our fingers smudged with centuries-old ink, and between us, in beds crawling with leafshadows, those books bled their contents and burned with magnesium flames. We climbed on roofs of buildings and hovered above crayon cities blanked out by war, with the constellations stenciled into the sky all around us. We breathed underwater and spoke to the sea turtles, asking them their opinions on the design of the new Temples at Mamasi and Papano. They answered us with ruins of sugar mills, forts, labyrinths, and the mazes of crabs' tracks making demented treasure maps in the sand. The reality of Anna's electric blue eyes and the footprints that laughter left along her temples and the whiteness of her naked skin could not be gainsaid—she was alive in me. I awoke in the mornings or the early evenings with no sign of how to reconcile one world with the other—until I realized—again—for the billionth time but as if for the first—that I could operate my quotidien life arm-in-arm with Anna, so long as I did not let the torture of my ecstasy, or the ecstasy of my torture, overwhelm me. When they did, I spent whole afternoons picking fragments of my skull off the rubbed plaster walls of my cell. I licked the backs of the fragments, their concave faces shone iridescent mother of pearl, and I pressed them into place like confetti into the asinine carapace of a pinata, to be exploded again. This is what it means to be dead—you plunge your lovers headlong into Hell. Where are you then? In Hell watching? In Paradise tooting the horn of fortune? In Purgatory throwing daggers at Epicurus? All dredging questions of this sort will turn up the toad of nihilism if answered too quickly. The key is not to answer them, to realize that the tails of the musical phrases the mind creates are little miracles in and of themselves. With conceits such as these I learned to dredge deeper into my despair without giving over to the paralysis of guilt or its sister anger (*Ira*), and what I learned in the depths made me from a man into an indomitable spirit lodged in my body for a time, and knowing there would be others.

"She is my angel."

This is what I see coming out of Joseph Turner's mouth, in his backstage reverie, just before he became Othello.

"She is my angel of life,"

Or,

"She is my angel of death."

He himself did not know, yet.

Who is Turner? Does it matter? I ask myself these questions. What does it mean for someone to matter? Must it be that no other could have taken their place? It must be. It must not be. It must be.

I left Federico aglow in the Martian light of his car, I marched down the alleyway to the back door of the theatre. What was I feeling at that moment? I was feeling the papyrus texture of the script, the domino effect of the words, the slant of the stage directions. I was feeling the buoyancy of my mind, how I drifted out like a skiff over the undulations of reality by the motive force of centuries old recitations. Shakespeare, my dear. Shakespeare. There is no way to test whether or not you will remember your lines, there is just a feeling of humility at the feet of the master. He speaks to you, you do not speak. The crowd billows out like a fallen sail rippled by pelagic chaos and illumined by the searchlights of the stars. The moon shines only on you—it shone only on me. I began.

What kind of girl is Desdemona? She is a girl of noble birth who murders her father's hopes and marries a Moorish gentleman with no learning but that gleaned from seven years of slaughter on the battlefield. Her father is in conference with some other Venetian senators, making war plans. There is word (from Iago) that the white ewe is being "tupped" by a black ram, but the father is in denial. Enter Desdemona. For those who find Shakespeare burdensome, I paraphrase.

Where have you been, says the father.

I have been shacking up with a particular general of yours, says Desdemona.

But this cannot be, says the father.

It can, says Desdemona.

No it cannot, and now that we're talking about it, you're coming home.

Too late, she says, I've married him, he foots my bills, therefore I take orders from him now.

Fine, says the father, please leave.

And she is free? Not quite. She binds herself to a new master, invoking *his* supremacy over her as her protection from her father's. The father casts her off, pronounces her dead, and returns rather perfunctorily to state business, as if his daughter never existed.

Is Desdemona a rebel for marrying the Moor? It must be assumed that in Venice, where global trade was the game, and the Mediterranean was one's swimming pool, such inconvenient pairings did exist as that between a high-born Venetian and an illiterate son of the windborne miasmas of the Maghreb, whose skin took its shade from the tumescent landscapes of Naama. The pairings were so common, that Desdemona's father did not need to consult his law books to research his daughter's penalty: the rollback of a life—death retroactive. By the end of Act Two, Desdemona has turned herself into another pile of eraser shavings in the birth rolls of the Doge.

After being banished, Desdemona asks to be spirited to the front of some battle, so as, ostensibly, not to lose sight of her newly-wed Othello. But when she gets to this so-called front, the battle is a naval battle, and her patron is not even there. Cassio is there. Offstage, she fucks him, and they fall in love.

To understand why this is such a certainty, and all Desdemona's cries of innocence a sham, you need to understand what amorous fulfillment does to a man. Act Two, Scene Three. Othello has arrived in Cyprus, victorious over the Turks. The first thing he does, in Cassio's presence, is to attempt to claim his prize: he has not yet consummated his marriage to Desdemona. The two trot off to bed, and Cassio remains, with Iago, on watch over the victory festivities as the Moor has ordered. Iago is into his cups, but Cassio cannot drink. "I am infortunate in the infirmity", he says, "and dare not task my weakness with any more." Someone starts signing songs, and Cassio slips into drunkenness, flies into a rage, and nearly kills Montano for suggesting that Cassio's "infirmity" should be referred to Othello. The audience spends the next three acts following Desdemona's strawberried handkerchief round the stage, wondering if those bright red spots are intended to intimate innocence or lost innocence, while the key to the truth of the drama lies in a single word: infirmity. At first, Cassio cannot drink. He cannot drink because he is already drunken. With what?

Go back to the first Scene of the Act, and find Cassio at his most eloquent. Othello's ship has been misplaced at sea. Montano and Cassio stand on the Cypriot shore, looking out. Montano asks, "is your general wived?", and Cassio describes Desdemona in the brightest light a poet can shine on a girl, that is, he says that her beauty and presence exhaust the abilities of poetry itself. She is "one that excels the quirks of blazoning pens, and in th'essential vesture of creation does tire the engineer". Then mysteriously, given his infirmity, he prays that Othello's ship might sail by the shoals and sandbars, the "traitors ensteeped to enclog the guiltless keel", so that the Moor might "make love's quick pants in Desdemona's arms". Why would he want to foul his own wishes so, to see his "perfect" girl encircled in dark and foreign limbs? Why would he hope that the love were made hastily? There is no explanation but that Cassio's seed is busy swimming up the guts of the "divine Desdemona" as he speaks. Who is his interlocutor? Montano—the same he nearly kills for threatening to tell Othello of the "infirmity". You would not kill a man for telling the general you are drunk, when the general's very herald has ordered "each man to what sport and revels his addiction leads him". So— my Desdemona is Cassio's whore. My interpretation is incontrovertible....

Turner was the man I cast as Othello. His dimensions were so perfect to me, that I would drool into the bedsheets as he tearfully did the bidding of his irresistible jealousy. He was a tall, built, hairy, super-human man with a shade of blood shot to his eye and an accent that made the words tumble from his lips as if they were being defenestrated. He had an adorable tic when addressing his Desdemona, namely he would raise his hand to his face and mat down an invisible moustache with his thumb and forefinger, it made me feel the nakedness under my clothes, as if his mouth knew my body and was about to rattle off the names of its plateaus and hellesponts, the compositions of the metamorphics and precious metals that slid through its veins. More proximately, it made me feel that his fingers were the two inner veils between my thighs, and that the next two words he ejaculated would trumpet up into my uterus and shake the apples from my trees. After this little movement, Turner would raise his flattened hand next to his face with the dorsal side facing me, as if to show me some scar he had received there. Now my pubic hairs would be standing at attention. The hand would pause in the air, in something of a confusion: to my mind he was unsure of what to do with his genius. And he was a genius. Each gesture, each glance he made was so expressive in all the right ways, that had I been the owner of his body, I would have blown off my own hands and eyes just to avoid overloading my own senses. Had he not fallen in love, the man might have been Broadway's dusky messiah. I do not mean to say I have remorse—Turner came to serve a much higher purpose than he could have done in the outside world—I mean to say, there was no understudy of Turner, he had the god given stuff that you cannot repeat through any sort of diligence.

On that night when everything changed, I sailed in widening tacks to and fro across the stage possessed by the moonshine. I did not speak my lines, they were extracted from me by the silences in the crowd. Intention had fallen from me long ago. I was a body wrapped inside a soul.

FIFTEEN

"I ALWAYS RETURNED"

I always returned November's correspondences, so that our chain of whispers across the deadlands of America was unbroken. My letters to her were composed, with one exception, on note cards, for foolscap was too numbing—why write a word if it was to be dwarfed into insignificance by a congregation of extras—and stationery was too uptight. Upon receipt of her letters, just to register my presence, I would send a tickler back immediately with the morning post. Then I would begin.

As the summer wore on, and my respect for my own solitude deepened, I cared less and less for the substance of November's writings. It was their appearance, her penmanship, their length, the timing of their delivery. First, I had to get up from my couch and look at myself in the mirror. The mere thought of getting up would push me into another hour or two of slumber and nightmarish dreams. Anna in her many forms, death in its many forms. A distant cousin, naked and preposessing, with a nipple the size of a little toe, engorged and ready, and water pouring over her chest like the final cleansing ahead of a sacrifice. Halls upon halls of an unknown mansion, a constant sunset on the horizon. I would search for some girl, it was always a different one, and upon finding her, I would discover an insurmountable flaw in myself. My teeth were falling out. My skull was shattered although still swimming inside its skin. My body was paralyzed. I was in the midst of a heart attack. Or she was not real—a flaw in my imagination. I would attempt to wake up, and thereby thrust myself into a second, a third, a fourth incarnation of the dream. Sometimes I heard voices calling my name so clearly that they were more real than my own. I would wake up next to myself and climb over my slumbering body to the bathroom, in whose place was a torture chamber full of Jesuits illumined by incredible light gushing through bronze casements larger than the space given them.

On the same day November's last letter arrived, I smoked a mountain of dope and I drove down to the beach. I saw visions of a girl named Lora, an apparition whom I had never met. She plugged my hand in the space between her legs, which so refreshingly tasted like juniper. She spoke about how she would never see another landscape so timeless, how she would never feel so gloriously suicidal as she felt on the dunes—and knew like an amnesiac fielding a childhood memory that her life would repeat itself in various forms—a booby—an egret—a buzzard—a dragonfly—and felt that we were composed of multiple souls—one in our fingers, another in our toes, someone in our gut, another one in our skull, just like that, making up our multitudes of attitudes. I walked the beach until I had far surpassed my fatigue. Men and dogs and men and women and women and children ran into the spray and were swallowed and yielded up again. I lost my sense of footing, regained it, and saw Lora in double, her glasses making eight eyes.

"I need to sleep."

She pulled me towards her, needful, inscrutable.

"I need to sleep."

Her many eyes threw out spouts of water onto her many cheeks. Her too red mouth made circles round her face, a maypole of want and unfulfillment. My legs buckled and broke, my arms wrapped around myself.

"I need to sleep."

My eyes closed, I could see that this phantom of a woman was in fact a compendium of many. I tried to chisel her, I tried to mold her into the shape and sound and taste of November, in vain. She evaded me by miles, by movements, by generations. The contours on the dorsal surfaces of her hands and feet, and the sunbursts of expression behind her eyes, told of the entire spectrum of human experience. Had she also seen death and resurrection?

"I need to sleep."

The phantom held me to her body as tightly as she could. I felt so numb that I could not identify the feeling as numbness. My mind lost its ability to evaluate its dominion. The machinery it supposedly controlled, a series of picture postcards making up its beginnings, the velvet curtain of the future—the coordinates that might have situated me in that place, at that time, in the guise of a man called Polonius, faded into the background as fireflies who have lost their ability to ignite.

"I need to sleep."

I opened my eyes to find myself on my couch with the whole of the girl-phantom's weight on top of me, a weight that felt no more ponderous than the body of a bird. I ran my hands from the crown of her head to the crown of her buttocks, again and again as if I were trying to smooth out the clay of an unfinished figure. Her apparitional breath fluttered in sleep. Her hand kept brushing mine as I fingered the faces of the carpet's shaggy squires. I could see from my position the letter I had retrieved but had failed to open that morning. The envelope was more taxed than it ought to have been, as if its contents had perished in route across the country and were bloated with putrescence. The flap was taped down, someone had opened it then shut it again. The address had bled as if having shed tears all the way from Conshohocken to Culver City.

My ghostly companion fled. I opened the door to the rear porch, everything out there was dark and ringed with grimy mist, everything scared the hell out of me—even the moon that hung in the sky like a Blakean sickle, ready to play hangman. I floundered over to the liquor display in the study. The owner of the house was a retired botanist, he did not seem to keep real books—his were just reinforcements making the walls thicker in this particular part of the house. There was a forlorn orchid in the window, a blown glass lamp hung from a brass chain. My papers were everywhere, as if someone had rifled through the desk in a wild search for my will. A portion of the bookcase, in which the spines of the *Britannica* were an austere and forbidding audience, lipped out deep enough to hold five or six good bottles. I picked an old rum that tasted like the stained surface of a mahogany dresser when first rubbed with turpentine. I imagined that the bitter taste of the liquor would hold me back from consuming too much of it. In vain. The contents of the house agitated off their bearings and hovered in space. Dish rags and microscopes and whole legs of Parma ham and antique lamp stands and slotted spoons all got up and joined hands and paraded in chaos through the rooms and up and down the staircase and swept up more accoutrements into their wake—bottles of olive oil and overripe bananas and pearl onions and library books and postcards from a village in Austria where a cousin was languishing. A ship in a bottle, a frankly oversized set of women's underpants, a fedora, couch cushions, a miniature statue of Apollo, the sickly moon. The living room was a nightclub of inanimate objects. The eyes of the subjects of the portraits that hung on the walls rolled deliriously. The parade slowed to a gelatinous crawl. Doomsday was among me. The act of standing on two feet became a mystery. Eternal and glorious human impotence. The world caught me up in its swing, my spirits violently elevated, I wanted only to get sober tomorrow and get fucked up the next night, my mind an old sock that ran every puddle and rode every laundry cycle and came out clean as a whistle, ready to be stepped on and shat upon once again. The immaterial Lora stirred, I fucked her blindly and heroically, and she dropped back onto the couch like a dead bird. Saw clearly once again, smoked, poured myself another tall rum, this time with some ice. Was I ready to read the letter? I was more ready to tilt a gun to my head and thirstily yank the trigger back. I opened the letter.

Dearest Polonius, it began.

I threw it in the trash, fished it out, burned a corner, tore it in two, pieced it back together.

Dearest Polonius,

You know,

I have been faithful to you. You don't know, you assume I have been profligate, I am telling you, I have been faithful. But for Rico and Elise—yet their chemistries are ours—yesterday I drank what must have been a liter of Elise's private blood. And but for the occasional this one and that one, for the sport. You know, Polonius, sport-fucking—bones on bones—refreshes the spirit like a good shave. Then I throw them away, disposable razors, to be forgotten and forgotten. There are my hands too, and the occasional immaculately curved zucchini I cannot pass up. This is the universe. I am fantastically flawed. My heart and soul remain yours. I cannot live, I cannot breathe, I cannot sneeze, I cannot sleep, my senses fiend for the image of you, your voice, your hands, I feel like a child starving for the teat of her mother—and nothing works, Polonius. Nothing works. Now writing this letter I realize that every morning I wake up and I cry over my coffee—if only for a split second, and I explain to my interlocutor that it is only my allergies, or that the shower water was so hot. Or that somebody died. I have run out of aunts and uncles, acquaintances, classmates, murders, suicides, grandparents, miscarriages.

There is no diagnosis but incurable love to explain my despair at your absence. There is no cure for incurable love, yet I have tried. If I take a tally of each day, I try to cure it first by sloth. I stay in bed for as long as I possibly can, until I have parched myself as dry as the bottom of an evaporated lake and starved myself delirious. The bad dreams resurrect in me and have their way with my brains. All have a thread running through them—a thing of beauty I cannot capture.

I rise, and it is nearly impossible to stand. I try to cure my fatigue with coffee—and I try to cure the useless animation of the caffeine with six or seven cigarettes. I try to cure the lassitude of the smoke with a sniff of cocaine. By this time my identity is a knot of addiction whose pain gives me the feeling that I have translated my desire for you into something concrete. The feeling of carrying a stone takes me through the working day, until I have the ability to re-embrace vice. As the sun drops below the meridian, I am raw with poison, putrid with failing, fat with self-restraint. There is a bathroom in the basement of the drama building, at the far end of a forest of plaster casts and costume trees and toy trains. The air down there is heavy with its own sense of sin. Black mold runs down the stone walls like the tears of a deposed dancer. Who got me into this circle of fifths? Who is going to get me out? How many are we, Polonius? And does it matter. The bathroom has no real venting—I imagine that the stuff of my past self-intimacies has fluttered out of solution and gathered like fairy dust on the floor. Here it often strikes me. Why do I not just go home and rape myself in the comfort of one of our finely tiled bathroom floors, on the cushion of so many forgiving towels, with a stainless-steel stream of water flowing in the background. Why do I need to do it in this hexed womb, fallopian with the blood of rusted pipes, defaced with the anti-art of so many wasted souls? They write messages to each other, solely in vulgarisms. This is the place where you are guaranteed not to be known or appreciated, guaranteed not to find what you are looking for. And therein lies the evil and the point.

I rape myself, then I go home in a daze, sort of happy, if such were a thing, because I notice at this point, on my bicycle in the total anonymity of the evening, the streets deserted and smiling back at me somehow, that I will never put an end to my suffering, I will just get closer to its origins, and be able to turn it about on an axis, like a child spinning the globe and expressing wonder at where she is in fact situated. I want you, I do not have you. I have you, but I do not have you. I cannot possess you, and I do not even want to—what then? I cannot let you go, because you are intertwined with my viscera. What now?

Is it fair to say that one thing leads to another. One thing leads to another. There is always Elise, and there is often, more and more, Federico. I think they both surpass us in their focus, their diligence, their systematic genius, she for the imaginary machines of mathematics, he for the sound of a vibrating string. Federico has started on the piano again, and in the smoke of his repetitions I see something quite apart from myself, a way to put an order to our daydreams—a discipline I will never master or even want to embrace—I fear it would invalidate the brightest of my ideas—imagine sweeping up your mind into a neat set of piles—or building it into a structure. But he manages. The bathos of fame has not gotten to him either, he is as scrappy as you can imagine. Maybe a little fatter, but when I look at him I decide that he is not even a little fatter. And Elise—one thing leads to another. We begin with the feeling that we are not truly different people, that we belong to one system of vessels. Passion presses us together in a circle and tries to give truth to the feeling. One embraces the other, the other the one, the one the one, the other the other, there is soon no real difference, and once we've imbibed each other's fluids and pissed and shat them out, our chemistries are interbound—including self with self—since I will taste myself on him and in her—like going diving in the sea and finding your double under an ocean shelf.

I wake up in the middle of the night, chilly or burning with a false fever. Inevitably I have had a dream whose emotional pressure has closed in on me so suddenly that it has spat me out into the worst of all possible worlds, the one where everyone and everything is playing dead. In search of pleasure I have robbed my body of the ability to feel. Boiled down to my essentials, my weaknesses, I hold my head in my hands and try to weep, and I reach for you.

All this to set the stage for what happened the other day, on the stage. Do I say his name?

I did a dance of overflowing fear and frustration and despair and drunkenness and crackpot disillusionment—this was the outward expression of the heart, whatever that is, being separated from itself—and it took all the strength I had not to tear the letter into irredeemable shreds. I took another shameful drink from my drink: it did nothing. Then I tore the letter into irredeemable shreds. Showered it everywhere. Took the sleeping phantom into my arms. She was more nuanced and more beautiful than I remembered. I awoke to find myself sobbing and coughing and retching drily over a passage I had pieced together out of the rubble. I had not torn the thing as well as I could have.

Somehow the morning found me on the couch, in a sea of literary wreckage. In the kitchen I found a jar of clementines. I thought to myself, smiling a bit mischievously into the abysmal sunlight, that Joseph Turner's poaching of my one great love had opened a trap door in my existence. I resolved to build myself a harem of beauties that would rival those of the great Khans. My body would never be without a set of oiled little hands and curled little feet, grabbing and grappling at its flesh. Hungover mornings such as these would be serenaded by women and girls, the cascade of the shower and the pull of the hairbrush, coated with the taste of last night's master blend of delicate tinctures, couched in memories of impossible mountain tops of orgasm after orgasm, untied and liberated by sweaty reenactments of the Fall—pleasure without ulterior purpose—life that cheated its impending doom. Or the mornings would be less bright—I would wake up with my face in the dirt of dehydration, my cock wallowing in its own stench and the blood of fatuous fucks, the clocks running breakneck for midnight, the streets uncrossable, the air suffocating, and the girls not the sort you wanted to wake up to. Either way, I was not going home.

SIXTEEN

"MY LORD, MY LORD, MY LORD"

"My lord, my lord, my lord!" I heard the girl cry, like a toad in a deluge. I don't remember who played Emilia. I remember forgetting the names of bad actresses, and women generally. I remember the flesh on her cheeks being divorced from her mouth, as if someone had fastened her face to her skull by a set of desultorily clasped safety pins, and some of those pins had come loose.

"My lord!"

Under the croak of the cry came a tremolo of urgency, as if I were still alive and she could still save me. I wasn't, I was dead. From the grave I could hear the air whistle and whisper into the collective chest of the crowd.

"My lord!". The pressure on my pillow bore down so resolutely that it loosened up my neck and unlocked random spirits from the cerebellum. I had the thought, too, that if I was not to drop right then and there through the floor of the stage, at least some kind of gravitational change was imminent. Was I going to slink off the bed like a mercurial cascade? Was I going to apotheosize? Either way I resolved, among thoughts of how small the universe must have been at its beginning, among thoughts of elephants and the sun multiplied and refracted in a sort of pyramidal mirror, that I would not fall out of character.

It was the scene where Othello drowns Desdemona in a sea of feathers. She confesses to her crime beautifully—kill me tomorrow, just let me live tonight—and he drowns her in a sea of feathers. But when Emilia, her maid, calls at the bedroom door, Othello leaves Desdemona in a half death, and the girl, or her ghost, sprites about for one final moment before, we must assume, succumbing to a heart attack, or flying heavenward. Turner and I had practiced the scene by now a good hundred times, for the choreography of dying and coming back to life is difficult to perfect without injecting slapstick into one of the most poignant apogees in world literature. I had learned to play dead and then, at the right moment and with movements like the fingers of a master at the keys his piano, turn around and play living. Those good hundred times I had felt I had gotten it wrong—you cannot know what impression you are giving the audience when your eyes are turned inwards towards the underworld—and a good hundred times, I now know, Turner had been suffocated too, by invisible forces at the sight of my behind staring up at him through Desdemona's diaphanous dress. I never wore underwear. My body needed to breathe. Even the finest fabric gave me a feeling of friction. My sex parts are not the sort that repose sleepily behind an ambuscade of flesh, they are evident, curious, on watch at all hours. Try as I might to keep them contained, they serve as my rudder and compass, my periscope on the world. I can even say, without exaggeration, that my pussy has a life all its own. This is my impression given my happenstance experience with mirrors. I never took the time to inspect myself as a scientist would, for fear that I would demystify the whole thing. And I surely hadn't seen myself from behind, as Turner now did, with my ammunition stacked against his senses and self-restraint. I noticed that Elise would spoil me a bit more when I was on my stomach versus on my back, and until I nearly drowned in that sea of feathers at the hand of Turner, I had chalked Elise's indiscretion up to her feeling of comfort and privacy, when I was not observing her at her labors. One does not particularly want to be seen, not even by one's own eyes, with one's tongue up someone else's ass. But I had underestimated the aesthetic, or the numinous, pull of my parts, the soft and severe, the downy hillocks cascading into two inscrutable rifts, both of which were

decorated by nature to denote both poison and sustenance. I had this hold on Turner, and he was pressing
the pillow over my head so resolutely that the entire
action existed outside the realm of acting. My face was
lodged in the mattress, I breathed the air from the coils,
it tasted like naphthalene and very aged cheese.

"My good lord, I would speak a word with you!"

I wanted to flail, my neck felt newly elastic, but I
had already flailed once and come to rest, I could not
break character. So the risks of the theatre, a place
where expressly nothing mattered, yet everything
mattered in ways that they never would on the outside.
The crowd began to exhale, and groan, and whisper
insurrection. Turner bore down. The wave of his weight
built and broke. Doorways opened inside my body. I
could feel the tautness of my skin, the hollowness of
my bones, each and every hair follicle I could feel. The
rondure of my eyes, the absurdity of my nose, the hollowness of my skull, the angle and openness of my hips,
the remoteness of my toes—so remote that it seemed
you would have to take an overnight train or a puddle jumper between them and my fingers. I wondered
why I needed two of everything. There was perfection
to carrying one thing in one hand, and another thing in
another hand. Holding a third thing under one's chin did
not make much sense. There was perfection to playing
a stringed instrument. There was perfection in holding

a book open like a buzzard drying its wings. I could feel the presence and strangeness of everything, as if one clock had been smashed and another form of time had been put in its place. That was the first doorway.

The crowd made a confused collective movement that shook the air around us. The moment was lasting too long. Turner droned his lines as if saying them only to me, and of course I could not hear them. His gravity continued to grow.

The second doorway. This door was heavier than the first, it took such force to open that I nearly let out a sound like the grating of iron hinges, a mix between the triumph of a flute and the moan of a cartoon whale who has lost his way at sea. But once I caught a glimpse of what was on the other side—like a lost half-god trapped inside a labyrinth who finally glimpses the dark blue gelatinous night sky above him—I let go. Pain turned to wonder, and even gratitude. I could call it pleasure, but it was not yet pain's opposite. It was pain's oblique. You see—you see!—I had not yet fucked this Turner. The not-fucking was a rare thing for me, especially if someone was my student. I always fucked my students, if they were willing, and if the timing was right. And even sometimes if the timing was wrong. I was the Chair of Drama—it was part of my duty. Girls, boys, girly boys, tomboys. But not Turner—not yet Turner. He was not for sport. He was too fragile, and by saying this I mean,

I was too fragile. I could not stand not to fuck him, so I did not. His frustration was my frustration—and the suffocation of my senses at his hand spelled symmetry.

The third doorway was Polonius. As quickly as the tension had left my body, as quickly as I was spirited to a mountaintop cottage where trade winds kissed my cheeks, so quickly the breezes became a hurricane, and the moon rose to reveal that all the windows and doors were shattered, and I was swept up into the arms of the storm.

He let me go, I played my ghostly part, and expired on the bed. The denouement took its drawn-out course. Ludovico said his piece. The audience exploded with relief that it was all a dream.

Later, on the way home in Federico's car, I told him. He hadn't noticed anything out of line—all he knew was that Desdemona was dead as an omen. Federico's eyebrows overtook his hairline as he listened to me. He put both hands to his face, prompting me to take the wheel.

"The demon forking passion has got me, Federico. I feel that if I do not go to him now, right now, this very moment, the remainder of my life will rest in a long shade of regret."

"How do you know?"

"Has anything like this ever been explained?"

"But..."

"But what?"

"You know what, or rather *who*."

"I don't know."

"You do know."

"But I am not his...."

"No you are not his...and I am not your...But I feel that you might be trading one shade of regret for another. There is perhaps no way back into the sunlight, from where we sit."

"In my heart and soul I have already been unfaithful. There is no turning back that clock..."

"In my heart and soul I have been unfaithful with half of Philadelphia."

"..."

"..."

"So Federico."

"So November."

"So what do I do?"

"I cannot tell you that."

"But tell me anyway, please."

"..."

"..."

"What is his address?"

Federico stopped the car and lit a cigarette. He smoked it, and lit another cigarette. The moment seemed to sprout tendrils, with the smoke tattooing the air. The lights of the dashboard made our faces into purple masks. Nothing played on the radio. There were night bugs. The facades of the old brick townhomes looked more alive than any person on the street.

"Second and Catherine," I said.

We drove down to the older part of the city, into a warren of small streets and alleys and miniature houses for the miniature men and women of history. Turner's block was poorly lit, and from the shape of his house, a modernistic yet rectilinear structure recessed from the surrounding facades, you could never have guessed the labyrinthine nature of the interior. Federico and I went in together. Girls and smoke and the notes of a saxophone floating around everyone's head. Close rooms where the air was nonetheless perfect: all the windows and doors were open to the summer night, and the seemingly rubix nature of the house let through all the cross breezes. Certain levels of the house were expanded landings of what seemed like an endless staircase. There were books everywhere, art everywhere, precious few places to sit, the place seemed to be made to envelop wandering spirits who drank on their feet and presumably fucked on their feet as well. I remember seventeen or eighteen bathrooms, or it may have been that I passed the same bathroom seventeen or eighteen times. Conversation touched upon so many fertile fields of thought, and Turner, knowing everything about everything, would discreetly pollinate a cluster of guests but draw away before one's attentions could narrow on him. From his measure-by-measure knowledge of the hard poets and the crusty philosophers, the deep novelists, the vagrant composers, the basement improvisers, and his ability to relate one to another across disciplines and across history, it seemed that he had lived since the last ice age. And his ability to rest silently and listen to us, let us have the time and space and safety it took to formulate a coherent thesis under pressure and under intoxication, showed that he respected everyone in his presence as minds on a level with his own, not merely as ears or corroborators. He ceded the floor to Federico for an interminable lecture on the Brazilians, and gave his input only as tersely accurate footnotes at critical junctures—so that the rest of the company could understand. He knew the month when Augusto SaoBenito was born, and he knew the ways in which the absurd Corolitan jazz of the '20s changed from atonal to tonal and back again without jogging the ear. He had listened long in Federico's oeuvre, and facilitated comparison between Federico's rhythms and those of the fantastical master Stephan de Ipanema. By this time Federico had become accustomed to his own fame, yet the ice in his glass did quaver next time he brought it to his mouth. Later, after the champagne had led to wine and whiskey and drugs, on a landing leading to a hawk's nest whence the bird calls of Turner's saxophone issued with effortless crescendo, Federico admitted his vertigo. He was on his fourth or fifth drink. His hair had gathered into a fish formation. Attached to him at the waist was an Estonian mathematician who was completely white but for the barely baby blue of her eyes. Her bearing left no doubt of an aristocratic heritage, and her nearly permanent smile betrayed incalculable loss and the forgiveness of everything that came after. Her parents had named her Tatiana. She had just done with letting Federico out of the bathroom, where I could hear them scuffling against the door for each other's affections. She was telling him that she considered geometry a universal language, and that she would dedicate her life to defining nine or ten dimensional space, in order to understand what the eye was supposed to be seeing.

"Vertigo," said Federico.

The saxophone grew closer. It was telling a story of the meaning of music. Ever elusive, ever a mirror of one's own consciousness, ever in orbit of a mischievous eye. The company stood in a circle around Turner and his instrument. Looking at him, I got a feeling of sickness, as if someone had poisoned me. I wavered. Tatiana took my arm in hers, I hung on her like an invalid. I took stock of the various parts of my body. The soles of the feet had gone numb, the hands and the elbows had gone numb. The knees and the chest and the feeling of my clothing on my skin had gone numb.

Strangely, I could not feel my sex parts either—it was not them that did it. I could feel my guts. With every breath it felt that my insides were going to turn themselves inside out. I had eaten something—but I had eaten nothing. The years themselves, all the years I had lived, wanted to come out of me. My vision blurred, the crowd of people dissolved into the shine of the saxophone, Federico handed me a drink, it helped, but only by making it more crystalline to me that I was in trouble. I lit a cigarette and asked him for another drink, before I let myself form any further thoughts. Another drink, another cigarette. The crowd swam from one reef of the room to the next. Turner's eyes were punched shut and his cheeks ballooned in blowfish flamboyance. Chains and flames and teeth and the spark of human fusing into human showed bright like sunken treasure. The lights and breeze of the city midnight heaved and tumbled into and out of the windows and doors—my ears tickled—my head expanded—I lost contact with the ground. Plastered against the ceiling, I watched the gathering change shape again into a horde of savages around a beast, their fingers tearing at their hair, and their minds driven all but insane at the reality of the life form in their midst—the fact that intelligence and mortality could invest such a creature. He seemed never to take a breath, the air flowed in through his nostrils as quickly as it hooted and cried and flared through the serpentine flask of that voluptuous instrument. The music told stories—of giant mountain ranges seen from afar as wrinkles in a sheet of cotton—or of the ions of our bodies seen from very close up as whole landscapes of monoliths and terrible storms—and everyone present seemed to understand those stories—they moved as the notes of a score, rising together and falling together, ducking and reaching and bridging each other and repeating their movements with Turner's repetitions, it was impossible to tell whether they were dancing to his tune or he was an organ of their collective consciousness. Turner's eyes were closed the whole time, he had no idea what or who was going on around him, yet he felt us all so closely, he could read us through his own entrails.

"Enough," said Federico.

And I felt the saxophone reach the leeward side of a crescendo and start to fade into the distance and into my memory. Federico had plucked me from the party and was dragging me down the stairs. He shed a rueful and whimpering Tatiana (never to be seen again), and silence and the sound of echoes and the protest of puddles being torn into shards of mirrored night came back to us.

"Why?" I said.

"No why," he said. "Just enough."

He led me through the rain to his car, which was sleeping like a puma in the side street, and he drove us home in a loud but controlled drunken hurry, the puma ran a wave of stop signs all the way up Pine Street, the rain poured through the open window and against my upturned face, the dawn was mixing with the night.

I remember marveling at the blue shade of the stone steps in my house, struggling against the inhuman strength with which Federico lifted me into bed, then closing my eyes and remarking to myself that I saw more on the inner side of my eyelids than I ever could in a landscape or on the face of a human situation. I looked back into my mind and saw the negative of the room where we all had surrounded Turner and his instrument, I saw the magnetic fields that suspended us, I saw the stars in the air and the black holes, I felt the weight and the weave of the ropes and ribbons that connected one to the other. A theme, a pattern repeated itself in the shapes, the textures, the colors that met my inner eye—the theme of counterpoint—of opposition—between high and low—needing and wanting—body and soul—chance and fate—the very theme that held us all in suspension, all this time, the one that kept us alive and waiting for what would be. I could feel, even at that late hour and at that far horizon of drunkenness, by testing my heartstrings for rhyme and discord, that Turner had shocked me alive, like the finger of Zeus giving storms—and rain—to a desiccated countryside.

When I woke up the next morning—a Saturday—a morning enclosed by tiny snowflakes of mist all dancing to the same tune—I made myself a pot of coffee and wrote a long letter to Polonius.

SEVENTEEN

"THE SKIES OPENED
THE NEXT MORNING"

The skies opened the next morning and dropped a rare deluge on my world. The trees were caught unawares, in their shivering resistance they looked especially tantalized. Flowers were vanquished. Pomegranates bobbed and broke free and rolled down the streets. People were caught in it, they continued shrunken, their hair ruined and their faces coated with phosphorescent glaze, their eyelids cried tears that were rendered anonymous and infinite. The fog carried the sound of the waves over the crest of the Palisades, they were forever approaching us. Screams of jays too laden to fly. Beatles buggered and slow as sloths. The rain was wetter than jumping into a pool, the water was forced under your skin, stuffed into your consciousness. I went outside dry and at odds with myself and slung over the shoulder of last night's intemperance. I came back a hundred pounds heavier, laughing and new. I dried off, stripped naked, and did it again. This time I lay down in the lake that covered the back yard. I looked up through the raindrops coming down in myriads of millions, they flashed and dashed in a conical projection of my tunnel vision, they riddled me like bullets, they wanted to bury me. They tried and tried and tried and tried. But they could not bury me. Instead they buoyed me up, and all the pain in me washed into the flood.

I watched them go—one unpaired courtesan stumbling after the other out the palace doors, their petticoats in disarrays of yellow and flamingo, their digestions all in knots from the cinch of the corset. And I thought, I had not yet lived a moment—before that moment naked and alone for once under the skies' pointillistic recasting of the landscape, I had not yet lived a moment of my life that had passed without some measure of pain. From the birth of my mind—the morning when I realized that I had the run of my own thoughts, and could direct their action this way and that, like a set of armies marching against one another—I had felt the motion of time passing as a mast groans and cries torture under the weight of the wind. While all the men and women on board see is a sail stretched against the sky like the sage cheek of a god, and the horizon neatly assembled in a watercolor arc of blue on blue—while the wheel is seen to rock like a baby in a cradle—the mast is on fire. This fire—the same that, say, afflicts me on the stairs of the library tower, when I realize that I am either too hungry or too tired to be the man I am supposed to be, and that I might as well give up, this being as good a time as any—pulls whole civilizations together and apart in my mind. Restlessness, the urge to go with the wind or against it, the inability to leap out of my keel, the shelter and the madness of captivity, while waving the flag of surrender. The sense that I am moving against the land but not against the sky or the wind or the water, and I realize that there are galaxies and constellations and particles and oceans and tremenda and sheets and sails of pain that hem me in and follow me everywhere, that guide me from one day into the next. Even when the sunstreams of joy line the gunwale, it is there—pleasure is very different from the absence of pain. The two (pleasure and pain) are almost indistinguishable in their highest throes. They are Anna and November, back to back and grating away without issue, the slap of skin on skin is the collision of the waves over the fingernail of the Horn, is the fiesta of storms that gather when the hemispheres of the mind exchange telegrams. There can be no one without the other, for the experience of ecstasy relies on one's awareness of death. But the absence of pain—the absence of pain is the glassy eye of the moon doubled in a midnight lake high in the alpine unknown, living by its own light—in that way perpetual, yet mysterious, unseen by any but itself, and mute as a monk who has gone brain dead while levitating. So, I lay in my watery bed on the lawn, and I felt the absence of pain as a stillness in which I did not even know the motion of the earth or my presence on it or anywhere. I knew the in and out of my breathing, the undulations of my ribs, the webs of my hands and toes, and I knew the glory of the insanity that rested behind my eyes, I knew the music of the blood that explored my spider webs and cul de sacs. I knew the intimacy of nature and its foreignness. I knew nothing of my past or future, nothing of the ways I had gotten here, nothing of how I was going to rise and what then, nothing of who my relatives were or had been, and nothing of life nor the ends of it, the end or the beginning or the purpose. Nothing of myself as I had known him—the philosopher, the loving sophist, the soft lover, the nose thumber, the fiddler, the bum, the god, the exorcist, the teacher, the sage, the I. In the place of myself was an almost limitless profusion of reflections of "Polonius" in the eyes and expressions of all the people I had known—including my mirrored representation—from the beginning of my time to the present moment. The first image, almost a dream—my father imploring, my mother crying, and both of them suddenly looking at me aghast that I might have understood that they suffered from penury—and on from there to the eyes of the girl who had sold me my things the day before, their improbable and bottomless blue foretelling her apotheosis, and her subtle communications of gratitude—or so I thought— for having received my mute and genteel praise. Over these two images, which were not separated in "time" at all but simply coexisted like two leaves hanging from the same branch, there was overlaid everything else, which also seemed to fall into two gravitational groups: the faces of girls whom I had loved, with Anna in their center, and the faces of those whom I had not, in whose dark, plumlike middle there rested my sisters. The first group was generally in a state of orgasm or fake orgasm or fraught and ecstatic anticipation, the second was glazed over with frustration and panic, their faces scrambled up so that you could not tell where anything was. Some individuals belonged inscrutably to both groups. And the situations that recalled them to my mind were never simple or straightforward. Sometimes I was strongly and unconditionally desired, even wor- shipped by these feminine forms, but my heart—the painted back of the looking glass—was secretly rotten and lazy and despondent. Or I was despised for some abiding sin, usually of mysterious omission, and my heart would explode with adoration in response, as if such adoration could be a rebellion against another's hatred. And at the center, there was Anna crying on the cold linoleum of the library floor, she cried over the question of existence, she cried over the hunger of faraway children, the desiccation or infestation or conflagration of forests, the tincture of rivers with heavy metals. She cried over the inanity of history. She cried over her own suicide.

I listened to Anna's voice. In a surge of dirty electricity, the pain began to seep back into my body. First the heartbeat, like the bleat of a faraway fire alarm. Then the sinews of my frame, the hunch of the shoulders, the paralysis of the ankles, the upper legs, the rusty iron revolutions of the stomach and guts. The gorgon's head of my hangover. The impossibility of capturing for posterity the feeling of the raindrops that formed and reformed at the tips of my eyelashes. All flowed back into place. And in their wake, the most funereal of all pains did trawl—my sense of time. I felt the friction of what was inescapable, and I felt the inevitability of what remained undone, like blood clots waiting in my extremities to travel brainward and take me heavenward. All of these pains, I reminded myself, served a practical purpose. One must stretch out, keep moving, feed oneself, take in the purities, wash out the clays and dirts. One must renew and remember and create reminders of the visions worth seeing again. But, I asked myself, were these the cues I wanted to follow, or were they simply the most easily interpreted—and what was there so mesmerizing, so irresistible about Anna's martyrdom? Would I remain in orbit of her gravitation for the rest of my existence? When I asked this question, the pains all flared up, they did not want me to be released out into the world and risk allegiance to other forces, they were too accustomed to the creature comforts of captivity. To die in tortured shelter was better than to live in ecstatic exposure. They cried out "Yes".

Meantime my soul whispered back that it wanted very badly to say "No", but it could not speak in certainties—that was not its role. My soul lived in a parallel universe fashioned by process of elimination. It knew that there was no such thing as a true thing or a false thing. There were no bright things and no dark things. There was no I and no other people—there was no such thing as a high impulse and no middling and no low—there was no tomorrow and no yesterday and no reality and no imagination. No such thing as one thing leading to another, and no such thing as chaos, no predestination and no free will. My soul knew that there was no such thing as he or she or it, and when the hammer came down it would not come down at all, but keep swinging on like the tides. There was no better and no worse. No justified and no unjustified, and no gray areas. No life and death, no risk and no reward, no St. Peter and no choir and no rocky outcropping where the philosophers sat and no dogs chasing you and no dogs to eat you, in the end. My soul knew that there were only the ones whom I loved and the ones whom I did not, and the ones whom I did not love did not exist.

I picked myself up off the ground. The visions faded, stars lit by the dawn. I swept the water from my face and covered myself up and walked inside, slowly, and shivering. I had a long shower and a blissful nap where I dreamt of a billiards game with Federico in a vacant resort somewhere in East Asia. Stray cats had taken over the place. One of them fell down a mineshaft and waved goodbye.

I woke up in very bad need of a drink. It was almost evening. I had a particularly generous drink, and it gave me the self-awareness, you could say, to call on the phantom Lora. I did call on her: she had been watching me the whole while from the kitchen, she had eaten all the lemons. The conversation was barely spoken, she appeared. My body raged for her. Apologies and for-givenesses, frustrations, fucks, fatigue. The grand gyre went round and around. The rain gave way to cool and calm, the sun set over the mountains and we went out-side to take an air bath in our nakedness. She lay on a lounge chair and spoke miscellaneously about a whole generation of writers on the heretofore undiscovered island of Nubu who wrote in untranslatable Creole. One of them had written, on a series of palm scrolls, a novel bearing such a resemblance to Moby Dick, even in its encyclopedic, idiosyncratic style, that, despite the fact that the author could not speak a jot of English, the Trustees of the University of California were offering him a position. Problem was, the man did not understand the meaning of "money". Another Nubian, a woman, had written a body of homosexual love poems so akin to Sappho, that she was being considered for the Nobel, and the Board was particularly drawn by the fact that she did not understand the meaning of "fame". I curled up next to Lora with my arm across her stomach, and although she was at most half my size and did not in fact exist, I felt far smaller than she. I felt she could contain me.

"The point is . . . " she was saying, and as she spoke I drifted into and out of sleep, ". . . the point is that . . . alone on islands . . . threads in a giant fabric . . . the arms and legs . . . minds, they want to . . . we reach for each other . . . radical theories . . . the halls of power do not dream . . . made up of filaments . . . further away . . . and the many the one . . . the eye is trained . . . two people who have never . . . changelings . . . the stones that were thrown over his shoulder . . . two different continents . . . that it wasn't true . . . the organs of belief . . . my mother and your father . . . prostitute . . . two prostitutes . . . myself and . . . whatever her name is . . . don't tell me . . . the fire . . . the fire . . . the fire . . . ."

I fell off a cliff into sleep for who could tell how long. I woke up clear as day in my mind while my body was still comatose, and I felt Lora's pristine and immaculate diaphanous chest heaving and fluttering, heaving and fluttering, heaving and fluttering under my ear. She was crying so hard she could barely breathe. The tears were pooled against my temple. I tightened my embrace.

EIGHTEEN

"I AWOKE TO THE REMEMBRANCE OF A DREAM"

I awoke to the remembrance of a dream. The light on the farm was heavily blue in the dawn, and the beeches in the yard wore coats of wet gold. As I walked the grounds I noticed that the paddock fences stood in crooked disarray, the posts and beams leaned on each other as if having swooned, and the path from the house to the barn was erased in places. The barn stalls were too clean to have housed horses in any but the distant past. I moved into to the tack room, my old schoolhouse. Chaotic jazz swirled about the walls like whirlpools of snow that refused to fall. The windows were open, but outside I could feel that the air was at a standstill, as if the room carried its own pressure. At the desk burned a candle, by whose fire my mother ceremoniously lit a cigarette. She said,

"I can't find the door to my mind. It is flippant and absurd, and evades me at every step."

I lay down on the cracked leather couch and looked into her eyes. They reflected another scene, with mountains rising out of high plains, and a thousand perfectly round clouds perched in the sky like blackbirds in the crown of a tree.

"And when I do find myself inside my mind, I am buffeted and abused by its storms, like a tiny sailboat. I cannot right myself to feel the world as it comes, I am feeling the world as it has come, will come, and may come. Your father is dead. And when I try to escape back into the empty space that surrounds my thoughts, I cannot find egress either. Downways lead to upways, sideways lead to straight ways, I try to beat down the walls, but they dissolve and lead me to other rooms, where I must hear the same news, again and again. Your father is dead. And the only voice I can hear clearly is his, he is mourning his own existence in the underworld. He cries, deafeningly and hilariously, he tries to build himself some momentum, to build exit velocity from that place. He indulges in regret over what he said to me last—do we have any more milk—and he wishes he had said something more weighty, to speed or to put off eternally my own demise, or to help me in this world of the in between. But he cannot. I cannot hear his words, I only hear his cries."

My mother threw the cigarette out one of the open windows. She pulled a trapeze down from the ceiling and began to swing like a parrot. As she spoke the next set of words her body was transliterated into a plaster cast of itself, except the cast had a thin moustache like an androgynous Lord Byron.

"Life and death, Cherry November. Life and death. I see a distinction without a difference. And if there are two categories, why can there not be three? I do not think nature as she stands knows numbers, or cares for them. Because your father is not alive and not dead, and I feel he is alive inside of me."

Her moving mouth and her twinkling toes were sprinkling plaster on my head, her scissoring legs cracked like glass. She was fighting eternity.

I awoke in six or seven other places before I awoke in earnest, into the most fantastical dream of the set. The sun had found its way through a slot in the curtains, and its diffraction caused the room to take on an undersea glow. Everything looked as if it had been polished or left outside to gather the dew. Federico came in, soundless, with a cup of coffee, he left it on the bedside table next to me and exited with a studied haste. The curtains swayed with his pulling of the door shut, the flashing and secreting of sunlight counted off the moments just as the passing of heady clouds up above might reveal then diminish, reveal then diminish a coral cave in the sky. I noticed that the light chose to illumine certain things—the glass on my dressing table, full of wine and dust, the face of my watch, numberless and long unwound, the jagged Baroque designs woven into the fabric of the ceiling and echoed in the doorknob and the frame of my mirror. My mind could have settled like a butterfly on one of those sights and amused itself with the innocence of beauty on the surface of things, but it was drawn to the silhouetted wall opposite the bed and the vacuum of darkness that sucked it down into an Atlantis of illness, a city built of everything in my past that was wrong. My body writhed, it could not sleep, it could not wake.

I had not done enough. I had not done nearly enough. For the ones who truly loved me, it seemed, I had done less than nothing. What had I done for my mother and father? I could not save them even in a dream, and I did not save them from their inevitable fate in life either. My attachments, my preoccupations, my genius even, had only sped them towards their undoing, because they could not reach me, could not understand me, and I was their only child, their only hope for spiritual representation in a world that was otherwise anonymous, cold, deathly, murderous. In the dream they tried—in the dream of my past they tried every day to find the harmonic on which we would all vibrate together— farmer, philosopher, and daughter—as the pianist, bassist, and drummer would create a smoky elation for their crowd. But we lacked a brass section—the sax, the trombone, the trumpet—where was our leader? Thanks to me, we were godless.

What had I done for those children of others, who had found me, embraced me, and nurtured my fla-grancies, promoted my bottomless, orgiastic vision of the day and night, forgiven my elusive affections and wavering spirit? Who had no original reason but cracked up fate to have their lives untraceably wrapped up in mine. I had dragged them to and fro across the city, hogtied and winched to the harness of a devil's ass, in service of my vices. How many nights had I led Polonius, Elise, Federico into gyres of fuckery because of nothing, because I could do nothing else? With the wealth that my great grandfather had sacked away with such inno-cent labor and purpose, and with a dreary habitude and an overgrown intellect derived from so many years of finding the outer world drab and incomplete and hor-rifying, I inspired them to the service of my appetites. Every which way I could, and two or three at a time, with all limbs working like warps and woofs possessed, I sucked them into me, so that barely anything but their bones and marrow remained. Federico and Elise did not seem to mind being disembodied, they treated my pas-sion unto death, our collective concupiscence, their nat-ural servitude like any other hygienic hiccough. When they fucked me they thrived off the total loss of their energies in a gyre of unrecognition.

Polonius was so fragile that the process broke him. He fucked me like a king that had been deposed, and on his vain flight from the capital had been waylaid, arraigned and subdued. It was his last dance, every time. So deep was his suffering in pleasure. And I loved him—I love him—whatever that means—so there was no way out—there is no way out.

What had I done for my students, who sat in defile each morning to worship at my feet, who droned out repetitions of the dead in hopes of earning my favor? I fashioned them into plaster casts of myself, by means of artful hypotheticals christened by the gold dust of fame. Notice that when one speaks of a literary character, one always uses the present tense, as if that character is standing right beside us. Hamlet *is*. Daedalus *is*. Mishkin *is*. By means of theatre, and with the bait of my own recognition and attention, I forced them to undergo the most extreme experiences known to man. And they played their parts with all possible energies, believing, I trust, that they were sheltered from the actual moral and physical consequences of being who the crowd believed them to be. What the actor never fully grasps, however, is that the actor is far more real than the acted—the acted has no reality at all except in the flesh and blood of their interpreters. And casting does not happen by force—no Lady Macbeth has ever been dragged to the theatre in chains to play her part. Considering the range of experiences that the actor could be having, in lieu of chasing tragedy on a stage (and tragedy is the only true theme of art; comedy is the marching band to tragedy's symphony), there is naught but a fine line between the rehearsal of a murder, the dry run of a rape, the ape of a suicide, and the deed itself. The knife may be plastic, the cock may be rubber, the rope may be slack, the names may be changed, but the intent, the malintent, is there. What could have been my intent, then, when I first set foot in the Department of Drama, hell bent on making it my Forum and harem? And what seed germinated in my mind when I first conjured up a sold-out crowd at the Academy to witness the drowning of a young girl and the accidental poisoning of an entire family? The curtain came down, the audience exploded, and between my legs the levees gave way.

And why, when I could have recruited a perfectly passable Desdemona, and watched the unfolding of my production with maternal pride from the wings, did I decide that season to deconstruct the role with such impish mastery, to straddle purity and self-defilement with such seeming ease? To whom was I trying to prove my duplicity?

I rose from the bed with unsteady foot. Drops of Elise's blood shone on the white of the bathroom tile in perfect little pools. Less innocent spotlets riddled the shower curtains and the edges of the tub, they clamored for the drain before I could interrogate them. I sent three or four salutary shots of bile after them, then I starfished in the bathtub and let the shower pelt me in the face and the body. Reason washed away, and with it all the questions I had just asked myself. In my mind I conjured, in a tangle of limbs and ecstatic screams illumined by the firelight of the underworld, the vision of Polonius and what must have been the dozens of women who were servicing his body and soul as I lay naked to the winds and wasting away in his absence far away in my false Paradise. They converged, the one with her black hair blinding his sight of her long nipple breaching his lips, the one with her legs winding around his body as the wrappings mummify the cadaver, the one whose eyes glow in the dark like miniature blue holes in the earth's barren skin, the one whose tears pooled in the hollow of her neck, the one whose infantine ass could fit in the palm of his hand, and he could carry her around like a miniature Mannerist lady Jesus, the one who walked in public with her holes so agape that the breezes moved through her freely, the one who dragged him to and fro bloodied in the desert and parched by thirst at the mercy of her Napoleonic mind, the harpie, the fat freak with the stomach that dragged on the bedding as she lapped against him like a heavy tide, the one who needed to tie herself to the bedposts and shove handkerchiefs down her throat and stuff her anus with vegetables in order to feel him, the one whose desperation grated on his heart strings and made them raw, the artist with her clays and earthy textures and rotten scents that stuck to him for days, the native who swallowed him and pressed her trumpeting lips against his pelvis for practice during her lunch breaks, the one who suffered from all forms of illness and for whom his gentle company was her salve and panacea, the ballerina who never spoke but to shout obscenities describing all the delicious things he did to her. And in the center, my Polonius made his world an expression of his addictive and insatiate imagination, he materialized his dreams. If you saw him from above, you would say that he was not free in a literal sense, he was bound to the textures and scents and the surfaces of the female form, he was a slave of his sex. Yet he understood deeply the relationship between a man and himself, that he could escape the dictates of his nature if he wanted to.

I cannot explain to you what it means to be a woman, because I have never been a man. But there is one incontrovertible difference between our sexes. The machinery of a man's suffering, the gallows from which he eventually hangs, exists outside his body cavity. He can relate to it, he can intellectualize it, he can put it aside for a time and say compose a symphony regarding the seasons, or a treatise on how decisions about life's aims are to be made in the most productive or compassionate way. But we girls and our corporeal existences are identical, there is no grasping ourselves from afar or above, we are furled together like the close threads of a cloud. Every novel ever penned, every song ever whispered, every piece of theatre ever put on, every epic ever dreamed, every opera ever attended by the courts of kings and queens since time eternal, every poem ever scratched out on the prison walls in blood, every portrait ever imposed upon rock or canvas concerns the mystery of the female form and its fusing of body and soul into one. So, I felt, lying in the supernatural stream of time described by the cascade of the shower, and reaching by the finger width down the shining face of my body that just began to materialize from sleep into arousal, that there was no such thing as freedom or free will in my life. I would never divorce myself from my self, and even in its dormancy my womb would infuse my body with fear and misunderstanding and all conquering power and eternal need. Not simply the want of an object, not Polonius' *choices*, but eternal need of something ever unattainable. And in old age, I felt, I would experience in a void what I once felt in surfeit. My whole life would be consumed by my body, I would go to the bitter end of every day wondering what or whom to stuff in there, and I would not have the tools of removal to say what or who was better or best. Something was better when there was nothing, and nothing was better when there was something. So, the pendulum of my sex.

In my own dark thus, and tortured thus, yet knowing well the torturer and the tortured, I engaged in a thought experiment, no less for entertainment than enlightenment. I touched myself. Nothing happened at first, this was to be expected. My fuse was long and serpentine, I began thinking along that golden braid. First Elise, and her drops of uterine blood. I noticed a progress. Then Polonius—ripeness. Then an anonymous violinist from the other night—I began to open up and feel the shower breeze in my thighs and a snake of warmth from my entrails. Then a French graduate student and his hammer cock—a painful detour. Then a snapshot of a very old amour taken from childhood—my first encounter—a girl who lifted me onto the tack table, the same my mother had used for a desk, and tongue-raped me until my utterances whipped the horses into full rebellion—I found my stride. Then Polonius—again—bloom. Then Joseph Turner—the imagined look on Joseph Turner's face as he suffocated me under Desdemona's pillow. My parts inflamed into unrecognizable shapes, and the doves warbling on the ledge flew away in confusion.

NINETEEN

"PHILOSOPHY WOKE UP DEAD"

Philosophy woke up dead for me that autumn. There was nothing left to write, and nobody seemed to care. All my subjects were dead. Morality, love, eternity, free will, and fate. I rented a house higher in the Palisades, so that my view of the ocean was unobstructed by tree or rooftop. The house had no garden to speak of, the hillside to which it clawed by its concrete fingernails was too steep and dry for any but the wild poppy and the baby palm and the live oak. A cockerel woke me up early in the mornings, but I never saw him nor heard inkling of where he lived, nor spied what hen or hens accompanied him. The house was composed of four levels, each westward gazing face adorned with a sail-like awning that filtered and textured the sunlight. On the lowest level there was a makeshift bar, and a pool full of rusty leaves. On the highest level there was a roof deck where one could rotate one's gaze between the insanity of civilization and the inanity of the beyonds. The living spaces were coated in textured plaster, and Oriental rugs of deep purple and crimson were hung on the walls, making the place seem inhabited at all hours by warriors, sheikhs, medusas, Krishnas, Dervishes, nymphs, Rapunzels, Leopolds, flowers, and flamingoes. The master bedroom was partitioned from the bathroom by a faintly mirrored wall of glass that was joined acutely by the wall of windows in which was pictured the waxing and waning of a big, blue universe. All the furniture and the towels and the sheets were stark white as this page, the gloam of the city lights painted the sky purple, and when I closed my eyes in bed I saw golden impressions of landscapes where the yawn of eternity leapt up from the horizon to contain me in a cradle of fire.

In the ten years since finishing my PhD (Conway succumbed to emphysema the night before the defense), I had published a few dozen scholarly papers and six books. The first book was published to horrifyingly raging accolades, for it was clear that not a single reader understood, or cared, what I was trying to do. They thought it was a book about the modern age, and I did not have the energy to argue with them. Tenure came one morning so inevitably that I was tempted to throw it back and see if I could make what was supposed to be the crowning achievement of my career more difficult. With tenure came from my peers equal parts respect and hatred, none of which concerned me. I cared about many things—among them the course of nature, the undulation of the earthly bloods through the veins of rivers snaked over the ground and tree limbs etched into the sky, the incalculable distance of horizons, the human spirit's embrace of the quantifiable and the infinite in the same instant, just as light may be both a particle and a wave—but the expression of my cares took two narrow forms: the act of writing, really the act of patience and the tuning of one's ear to an inner music, and the act of resting from writing. These were my actions, two. All the while time flowed into me and was dammed up into a rambling reservoir of all that I forewent. Alone in a vitreous eyrie that screamed for engagement with the essential elements of life, I craved the release of my pent-up gravitation.

My first step, which I never finished and will never finish even when my charred corpse is torn to shreds the by the bloodhounds of Hell, was to mourn the passage of time. Let me take up a particular remembered day, beginning somewhere in the middle of the night preceding the sunrise. She entered my dreams. There was a party assembled around a table, in an architecture that combined the postmodern with the Medieval. A gaping fire flickered in the background and sucked the chill from the cracks of the terrace doors. Servants bowed and took their leave. We and our imagined friends and family, none of them recognizable, feasted on river trout and game and a mountain of hearts of palm. Domestic animals scoured the carpets for bones, and parakeets flew pathologically into the mirrors and debased themselves and their images. The company dispersed, and November and I were left alone. She wore a translucent black dress studded with gold stars. Her black hair was painted slightly scarlet in the firelight and was let to run in circles around her neck and shoulders. Her eyes shone deep greens and baby blues and rusted oranges akin to the palate of an impressionist sunset reflected in the sea. I approached her, she stood up, but before we could embrace, those eyes were fogged over with grey, and we both dissolved in miserable tears. The gouts and screams of despair suffocated us, and we died in each other's arms, among the dogs and the cats and the bodies of the birds.

I awoke, still howling.

The darkness in my room was molasses so thick that I could not tell if I was alive or under the ground. I felt November drift away from me a thousand more times before I made it to sleep again, and I woke up battered as a seaman who after forty days adrift in the doldrums has eaten his comrades and drunk his own piss and arrived on the arid shores of the Galapagos with no water in sight (the Galapagos, the gruesome twister of life's spine, the final stage in devolution, when we lose our ability to fly, where we grow turgid and slow down to the crawl of the tectonic plates). I found myself in the atrium of the underworld, the exhibition hall of spiritual holocaust, a primer on totalitarian self-destruction, the hyperactive cloaca of the earth. I lay in bed paralyzed until I was dehydrated and starving, and I could not gather the strength to get up and feed myself—therefore remained in the bed for far longer—until the growing tide of nausea rejected me from the horizontal and spat me up into the day. Everything hurt, from my mind to my brain to my skull, down into my guts and the linings of my body cavity, my throat, my eyes, my fingers and toes, my hips, the elbows, the flanks. I hobbled down the stairs. I feared I would involuntarily surrender my sense of gravity and go careening through space and down into the void. I bounced off the walls like a caricature of myself. When I arrived at the bottom of the stairs, a grey, frayed and punctured and bleach-stained rag looked up at me from the middle of the white tiled floor. The maid was somewhere. My spine rattled with tension. I could not bear the fact of another person in my midst. I was horrendously naked, my hair and body and pubis unkempt, and my cock dragged behind me on the floor with lassitude. I rushed for the sink and drank great quantities of water. The maid popped up from under the kitchen table. She saw me. She covered her mouth, and her eyes nearly dropped from her head. I didn't move. She knew no English, I knew very little Spanish. We looked at each other, she made a face of mock disgust, and we laughed until the tears marked our faces. I took a plastic bag from under the sink and filled it with Coronas, ice, a cantaloupe, and a jar of peanut butter. I moved up the stairs and hid myself behind a locked door. I made it to the bed to drop off my parcel, then dropped blindly to my hands and knees. My body was struck by hammer blows of despair, one after the other in such quick succession that I could not breathe. I opened the windows and gasped out onto the terrace. The sun was shining. My eyes were so drowned I could barely see it. I let loose inner screams brought on by the mind-scrambling feeling of impossibility. Anna in the form of November, November in the form of Anna, Anna in the form of Anna, November in the form of November, and face-less feminine beasts with names as familiar to me as the two I knew and had lost, appeared to me and held me close to their chests and were gone, in unending procession. The feeling of closeness to these phantoms was as palpable as the sensation of an entire cenote of fresh water touched to the lips of your Galapagos castaway. As quickly as I could extend my imagined face to taste November's lips, the water dried up, and I kissed the sun baked volcanic sharps of a badlands.

I had the feeling, never before equaled nor after, of my soul being wrongfully inserted in my body. I could not imagine living another moment in that state of self-rejection, nor was death a solution: In death I would be turned inside out, and I would be the wrong body inserted in the wrong soul, ever to wander at Euridice's heels up and down the pike of the under-world. I dropped my chest to the ground, a thousand pounds weighed on my back. I could not move, I could not breathe. Finished.

The maid stepped over my body. I saw her change the sheets (white to white), secrete the instruments of intercourse on my bedside table, take the spittle from the mirrors and try to wipe away the wall of glass separating us from the morning. I saw grains of sand dance out from under her broom. I saw her diminutive feet lodged in a pair of loafers, and her coffee-colored calves that swept up and away into the unknown. I closed my eyes. Draculan nightmares poured into my brain. A blanket was draped over me. Silence.

I awoke again. My cheek was so dry it had adhered to my teeth. The blood in both of my hands had ceased to circulate. I hacked them at my face and tried to get them to pull at my flesh, they brushed over me like branches thrust by a gale. An amoeba, I squirmed towards my bag of provisions. I clapped my dead paws together and raised a beer to my igneous lips, lapped it up, let it wash over my face. A word took shape inside of me, much like the first conceit of a newborn lashing at his mother's protruding teet: Again! I took up another, my hands electric with static. The colors started to fade back in. The white light breathed blue and exhaled gold. The shadows formed in the fold of the bedspread the maid had draped over me made a neat line of point breaks around my knee. Very well. Again! I belched and produced momentous flatulence. Flatulence, I reflected, was the surest sign of life. My chemistry was reclaimed. I took a victory parade to the bathroom, the only activity that made me feel better without asking anything in return. I stayed there for a while. Smoked three cigarettes. Read a good deal of a relic women's magazine. Ideas, albeit in nebulous forms, started to come to me. Ideas that had to do with the nature of ideas. Common ideas being the most power- ful yet the least true, and the least valuable to the indi- vidual in his own life; and specific ideas, original ideas, being the most rare and the weakest, if you were try- ing to rule a populace, yet all-conquering to the mind of the beholder. Like porcini mushrooms or elegant, deadly snakes that can only flourish in the wild, can- not be cultivated or tamed. Or not alike to such things at all. We may define rarity as a concept that in and of itself defies definition, positive or negative. You can predict the birth of a great thinker but you cannot predict the bent of his mind. The same impediment prevents us from identifying our own originality, when it may be right under our noses—or it may not be. People who know for a fact that they are original are most often postal clerks, baggage handlers, truck drivers, broom pushers. Bowled over by their own genius—or stupidity—we will never know. The ones who shine the brightest are often just humble enough to keep trying, for they doubt themselves always a little—albeit not too much to sink their schemes altogether . . .

I recalled the first time I had experienced the feeling of infinite recursion in the mind. I lay in my bunk-bed in a room with three of my siblings, listening to them gleefully talk each other to sleep. I was perhaps eight or nine. Infinite recursion: I realized that I could expand my mind by a hundred light years out into the imagined unknown once a minute, and I would never get to the end of it all before I died. What was "it"? The tremendum of time, the sense that I was freefalling down into the ages, and along the way my skull would strike a rock, without meaning and without consequence, just like that, a sound—and all would go on as if nothing ever happened—this sense of the wide waste of existence and nonexistence would shock me into delirium. All my thoughts, all my dreams—where would they end up? After my body was gone, where would I be? I had to be somewhere. Is it thus fear, or vanity, that makes the artist, or is it not vanity at all but love for one's surroundings and one's family, the simple fact of existence? Or does logic, meaning philosophy, have nothing valuable to say on the subject, and it is not vanity or love at all but an unnamed element inside of us, an electric charge or fissile force harkening back to the birth of the universe that leads us to seek and even affirm immortality?

I got up off the toilet and immediately felt ill at ease in my own skin once again. Before I could indulge in more sadness or confusion, I put on my running shoes and ran out the door. Within my first few steps, my path took me straight uphill and dangerously close to the sun. A plume of toxicity was scraped off my sea bottom and kicked up into my brain. I kept going. Civilization disappeared. The sweat came bubbling out of my skull and scrambled my vision. Naked scrublands gave way to a cooler, shaded clime peopled with live oak and sycamore. I passed an invisible milestone that told me I was at least part of the way out of my sanity. I kept going. The pleasure of being among the things of the earth shot through me with each rattle of the pulse; the pain of being human was trundled back to the lungs for its metamorphosis. Forgetting — remembering — forgetting —remembering. I kept going. I moved beyond thought. The trail reached a promontory and a view of the mountains above me, the sea below, the smiling blue sky. There was another runner up there, he resembled a mountain goat. He exclaimed something enthusiastically in an unknown tongue, much as a goat would do, and scrambled off the trail into the hills.

Satisfied that I had gone far enough, I returned home. When I got to the front door, I had a lopsided headache that made my eye socket feel as if it was wrongfully penetrated by my eye. There was only one choice. I restarted my inebriation. Mercifully, there was no one there to watch me do it.

Deeper into the afternoon, I began to get a feeling of my direction, my bearing on the world. My youth, defined as it was by the love affairs of my youth, was over. Love affairs with the power of the word, the thought, knowledge, which can take the shapes of idols. Love affairs with the intellect, which, I now understood, was the child's way of communing with life. Even the grown up philosophers, the De Sades, the Nietzsches, the Flauberts—so long as they spent their time *philosophizing*—that is, projecting their own feelings onto other human beings—they drew on the same logic that a child traces in his notebook, when he realizes that one side of an isosceles triangle relates to the other two in a certain way no matter how large you draw the shape. He envisions one the size of a pinhead, and one the size of a ship. But he has never been run through by a sword, nor has he been drowned in the ocean. You can make a set of fairly neat rules about life before you've lived it (or in the absence of having lived it). Hence Kant. But you cannot make rules out of your experience.

My direction, my bearing drew from a place beyond thought, beyond reason. It was, and is, a sense and an instinct of life as infinite and therefore indefinable. Single individuals, single ideas, appeared to me as so many points of light in a depthless cosmos. To orbit but one of those scintillating apparitions, be it a theory or a soul, was tantamount to planting a blade of grass and calling it a garden.

I opened one of my notebooks to record this new conceit, this sense that the mind and spirit, if they were to understand the universe, must embrace the concept of errant motion, of uncharted wandering. As I fanned the pages to find a blank sheet, I noticed a phone number written in November's unmistakable hand, and next to it the words "if you need help". Without thinking, I called the number.

"This is Jackie."

"Jackie, this is Polonius O'Mara."

"How can I help you, Polonius O'Mara?"

As she uttered those words, I felt time collapse over me so swiftly that its bookends, call them Homer and Hitler, boxed my ears. I felt a deliquescence in my skull, akin to that we must feel when the aneurism bursts and the blood floods our minds. An enlightenment took hold of my body. How much was I willing to admit to the world, now that I had opened the door to my consciousness that crack?

"Polonius? How can I help you?"

"With my dreams, Jackie. I have the feeling that if I do not live them out, I will perish."

"Cryptic. Very cryptic."

"I know you know what I mean."

"I only know what I can glean from your books, Polonius, and that is dangerous stuff."

"Think about your dreams, Jackie. Yours. But not the ones you have involuntarily, while demons with faces of jack asses are having a carnival with your mind. The ones you have while you are awake. When you are truly awake, truly alive. Alone, without any sense of being watched or your actions known to anyone, even less to history. The things you must do, the things you ought to do, the girl you are expected to be, the image you measure yourself by, all is thrown out the window. You have tried to throw yourself out the window, but that was the one thing you could not do. You throw your mind out, you extract it from your body and fling it to the gods or dogs. You remain, anchorless, not in air or on land or on water, without an element even. What do you dream? Whom do you see?"

"…"

"…"

"Polonius?"

"Yes."

"Where are you calling from?"

I told her, and she hung up. Hours later, when the light had withdrawn from the sky and I was close to fading from every form of fatigue and had walked in concentric circles for ages wondering what to do or not do next, a tremendous flashing of light blinded all the mirrors and windows, and a beast pounded on the front door. It was she, and hordes of her compatriots. They stormed in like an army of brutal insects and took over the house, coopting everything in their path. The spaces were shot through with neon light and the movement of dark dryads. Someone's black behind traversed by apron strings took over the kitchen. It produced cucumber salads soaked in yoghurt, casseroles, a stew sugared with polenta, and grilled lemons that were destined to garnish a punch bowl of mezcal, tequila, and other hallucinogens. Candles flared up on every surface and projected our wavering ghoulish figures on the plaster walls. A set of speakers shook the sheets of glass that led to the balconies. Two mustachioed policemen stopped by, entered, frowned, smirked, blushed, were offered a drink, withdrew to change out of their uniforms. A period of wandering followed, and I got myself drunk while talking to no one. I next spotted the policemen's bulked and exceedingly hirsute bodies in the pool, they were overwhelmed. Laughter rose in mushroom formation. Animal forms pullulated. The surrounding scrub on our hillside was shocked and illumined and could not hide its eyes. A beast with thirty backs was whipped from nature's brush. The forms wrapped around each other and themselves, they turned inward and outward at once and were transfixed, the consciousness observing itself as a plume of smoke in a house of unfaithful mirrors. I went back to the kitchen to seek something. A drink and a smoke did nothing to fill the hollow in my spirits. I sought the most remote and forgotten corner of the house, where I could sleep. Sleep was elusive. I remember the sound of pleasure becoming the sound of death. My face. My hands.

When I had surfaced out from under the first wave of sleep, where I had dreamed of flaming tortoises arriving on a beach in the nameless Tropics, I opened my eyes to Jackie's. They were two shallow black pools. She was not smiling, her business was not one of joy or redemption, her eyes said, it was one of digging deeper down, in order to get out the other side. It was rough going.

Morning. I awoke in a bed so involved with bodies and body parts that I could not tell who belonged to what. No one stirred. I extricated myself. I hopped into my clothes, nearly impaling myself on the bedpost, and

I slid out the kitchen door, along the side of the hill and out a path down to a ravine. I took one look back at the house, as if I had set the place with explosives and was about to give the signal ordering detonation. I turned back to the path. Using the dusty roots and rocks lining the trail as my map, I tried to envision my escape. I would go here, then hitch a ride to there, and thence to even there, and then past there to there and there. I had done what? Who? When? I did not dare utter why. And before I could file away my plan and continue walking, Jackie, naked as the morning light and running barefoot as Mercury, gathered me up in her firm grasp and wiry arms and dragged me back. She said,

"Polonius. A philosopher, my philosopher. You never know what lies inside you until you smoke it out. Not on the page, not in the comfort of conversation. The word is a false friend, until you can look back and rest assured that you have done all you can possibly do, in the world. When will that be, Polonius? When will that be. I want you to think about all the times you made things up, you invested the world with your fears, your passions, your peculiar inhibitions. Like that line in Desire when you say: Since no person can be verified as greater or lesser than any other, there can be no true dictates, no true rules, no true imperatives. Even anarchy is invalid, as it is, in and of itself, an imperative. Disorder is a strict imposition across or against the grain of instinct. There are no true guidelines but for the internal voice of the individual, which is made up of infinite other voices, a cacophony of claim and counterclaim. You are so confident, Polonius, but what if even you go too far? Or not far enough. You've got an anthill, you've got the ants with their meaningless signals—go left, go right, stay center, turn back. That's relativism, right? Meaningless signals, all, because they cancel each other out. You've got the ascetic and the profligate. The mendicant prince and the warrior priest. Billions of voices such that when you back up far enough to capture them all in a frame, you're already in outer space, you're already dead. What good is a philosophy that is so vacant it kills you—after so many heroes and villains have tried, over these ten thousand years of civilization, to root out meaning, burn it, sink it, bury it deep under ground? What good if, Polonius, we have forgotten the raisin, the figment, the impetus that lies at the center of all this."

"The raisin, the figment, the impetus at the center meaning what."

"The fat, stormy, impetuous, irresistible raisin meaning the queen."

"The queen?"

"The queen."

I listened to her all the way through her thesis, until she was satisfied that I understood her. I did not know at the time where this experiment was headed, did not know with whom I would become obsessed and with whom embittered, nor how the experiment would end. Would we all need to starve, or kill each other? Was a meteor going to strike us for ascribing innocence to ourselves? I looked around—at Jackie—at the desecrated sheets and floors and even walls—at the seven or eight of her compatriots, of all different dimensions and hues and poses and attitudes and sexes, everyone's eyes equally glazed over with confusion and relief at their nakedness and ours. I thought of saying something. But somebody touched me, and that was the end of the morning's coherent speech.

TWENTY

"I EXHUMED MYSELF"

I exhumed myself from the bathtub. My lips, my feet, my fingertips looked like they had been burned by a white heat and would never heal. When I came back into the bedroom, still naked and still steaming hot, Federico was sitting in one of the armchairs with his guitar, bent as he always was, and cross legged as he always was. He held a cup of wine for himself, and he indicated the one for me that he had brought what seemed like hours earlier. He was playing Flamenco. Up and down the neck, and side to side, and forwards and backwards, fast and slow, sticky and fluid, low and high, and then there wove together combinations of this and that, that and this, in webs that made something fantastical out of an otherwise anonymous steel grey light describing an unidentifiable time of day in the blue space of the room. As I listened, I saw the deep hues of the countryside in fall. I saw small animals and birds running along the forest floor. This way and that, this way and that, looking for each other in opposite places. I lay down on the bed, on my stomach, and rested my head between my arms. There was a brutal descent into a dream. We (who knows who, exactly) were on a roof, in a city of eastern Europe. Eastern, because the railings and the flashing were riddled with rust, and steam pipes snaked everywhere. We were trying to get from somewhere to somewhere, and we were under fire. Bullets bounced off the metal and brick and buried themselves in the softer flesh of the buildings. Somehow we were never going to get where we were going, and we knew it.

I rubbed my legs together like a cricket. The complex between them was tender and inflamed, I could feel that my lower eye peered up at the world with teary longing. I had tried to take care of her in the bathtub, I had indulged her in all the images I could conjure from the screening room of my mind. Turner, even. Turner! But all that business had left her—and me—feeling emptier than before. A void materialized, it yawned from my coccyx, around the cape of my body, to my stomach and my throat, the space writhed and shivered like a droughted forest subjected to an ill wind. The leaves crackled their lament. No rain could soothe them, only the fury of fire and regeneration. But then—once I was laid waste—only the rain. And over and over again, never to be sated, on a wheel of desire and perdition. Not even death, I reckoned, would untie the cycle, unbind oneself from oneself, for in Hell one was continuously immolated, and in Heaven showered with gluttonous praises that piled up like hail on the paradisiacal plain. Nonetheless, I longed for finality. The orgasm to terminate all orgasms. Who was going to give it to me?

Federico saw at least the carnal aspect of what was happening. Like a seasoned and patient old bearded miner he dug spade by spade into my inner stuff. He scratched away at my walls, dislodged all sorts of glowing and radioactive ores, gave freer rein to the subterranean springs and streams. I pressed my palms against the headboard, and he fastened his fingers around my heels. We made a rudimentary dynamo of energy, and a frozen fever trickled down my arms into my torso and pooled in my center. My body congealed, cracked, shattered, my face contorted into the tortured laugh of a gargoyle. The fever spanned outward, it made my belly feel that it was pregnant and about to burst, then it calmed again and drifted like a manmade lake pushing ducks around in circles for recreation. Federico felt me relax, and his motion quieted down to a whisper. He feathered the little mat of soft hairs in the crux of my back. My mind wandered. I saw the curving, maple

and birch-shaded, autumn leaf-strewn street sweeping up and up, past a rusted, rambling white Victorian
house where I, childish I, had dreamed one day I would
live. A simple existence, with couches, cats, and children all just slightly distorted in the leaden glass. The
autumn of my dreams was harsh, windblown, but also
of a freshness and a sense of renewal that spring could
not bring. The house was prominent but hidden, shaded
heavily by the oak or sycamore or chestnut that dom-
inated its front garden and porches and dropped its
acorns, or figs, or nuts all over the place. Nothing in
the house was ever a thing of perfection, there were no
maids or servants to clear our plates, no groundskeep-
ers to mow the lawn or weed the beds, it would be, so
dreamed I, silly I—it would be a labor of strong affection
for me to spend my days in the background, in support
of other lives more precious than my own. My husband,
a clever but reserved man, would come home from his
job at the local university, and we would light a raging
fire and play at rummy until the kids fell asleep where
they sat. Over the piping heat of the radiators the windows would remain open, and the sounds of the night,
the laughs of the crickets and the howls of coyotes and
the hoots of the owls would populate our room as we
slept, he and I, entwined. So the vision had gone in my
childhood, and so it went for me today without my
realizing that I carried such dreams with me still. I had

let these dreams collapse into my reality and become my landscape, indistinguishable from the siren call of the ambulance, the lantern shades of so many opposing eyes that glared in the street night, the redefinition of sunset through a pink factory plume, my drawn shades and my spirit lying tepid next to me in a cup-and-saucer, in its pot-shot drugged desuetude. You see, the spirit — by this time in my life, I had wanted to kill myself a thousand times. Why had I jumped into the river after Polonius? Was it to save him? I do not even know what was in me that night, what troves of loss, what lifetimes of lament—at what—at what? I never had anything concrete to lament, I never had an excuse. So I lamented the most terrifying thing of all—the passage of time. Better to have lost a lover, a brother, or a dear friend. Better to have paid with one's first born! Better to have given over one's lands, one's moneys, so to speak, to an overzealous tax man. But no, but no! I would never be bereaved out of order, I would never be reduced to any sort of penury. The funds my father's father had left separately to me, in addition to his townhome where I was so many times fucked and fucked up, in addition to the Treasury bonds that magically paid my necessaries, in addition to my tenure that would support a family of six, made such a glacier, such a theoretical escarpment of protection against unhappiness—there were no excuses—except that the absence of distractions led me, from a very early age, to stare death in the eye and know him intimately.

But why did I jump into the river after Polonius? The truth has so many faces, and even the skin of one face is tessellated with unidentifiable hues, pockmarked with symbols for which there is no Rosetta. I invent the truth, as I invent myself, and our identities are ever shifting into and out of equilibrium. She and I are two actors on separate stages reading from what we believe is the same script, but we will never know, and we cannot hear each other's voices. Knowing her is a feeling that my voice is striking a harmony with something on the inside. I rode over the bridge, I made tracks in the clean blessing of ice falling from the sky. I remember looking under me at how my tire etched its humble track in the snow. Anna Delancey—she did not strike me as Anna—she struck me as the other end of the alphabet—Zola. She ran towards me. The way she moved made me fantasize about taking her body into my arms and seeing about the point where her waist met her hips. Her hair was encrusted with snow. The wind took deep breaths and blew the bottom of her dress open. The wind kicked up and turned the world sideways, I focused on riding, lest I blow into the street—and she was gone. In her place was another spirit, I cannot describe his state from any sort of objective perspective, and if I could I would not, there are certain areas where words are of very little use. To me—to me he was my brother—and although I would have liked to rescue Anna Delancey for my own curious purposes, I dove into the river after Polonius so that he could live. I wanted him to exist, just as I might want a landscape to exist, or a painting that captured that landscape to stay safe. Polonius in the beginning, I would die to know him again in this way. The look he gave me, as he mounted the parapet to leap to his own certain doom, as he gave it all up for no reason other than fate, as he went fearlessly into the unknown.

Federico was trying. His cock was rifling through the secret places inside of me. I tilted my pelvis towards the ceiling and raised my voice in agony and held that pitch until Elise's approbation and applause could be heard, all the way down in the kitchen. Judging from his prodigious release over my back, Federico had reason to believe that he had given me the orgasm to end all orgasms. He collapsed, and I lay inside of his crescent shade. Nothing moved. I waited. For a precious span of time that I still remember as if it happened a moment ago, I felt liberated from desire. I do not know if this feeling can be communicated. The image of the priest strutting the paving stones of the Vatican, the image of the monk kissing the ground at Angkor Wat, the image of the lotus eater with milky white eyes, the image of the shaman, the mountain, the albatross.

Nothing and no one can serve as a representation of that feeling. I harbored nothing—I hid nothing—I held back nothing—and my perception of the world was of pure and perpetual becoming—everything forever being born and reborn—the colors and the shapes having infinite depth and infinite variation—and infinite stores of energy and movement.

What mistake did I then make? Was it to draw my attentions too far inward, such that my breath took on the intensity of a hurricane? Was it to shift my body in an effort to waft the sensation up and down my spine? The microscopic movement was involuntary, but it engendered in my mind a wish: that this feeling of not wanting anything would amplify, would flourish, would repeat itself: that it would last for the rest of my life.

When earthquakes occur under the ocean, they give rise to a pulse of energy so monstrous, that the resultant wave sucks the water off the beaches as it builds offshore. To the beachgoer, the introduction to a tsunami is the sudden disappearance of all the old waves and the withdrawal of the ocean to reveal the naked calm of a beach the size of the moon. It is not uncommon for villagers to explore the newly uncovered landscape, to gape and marvel and religiously wonder at its provenance. Then on the horizon appears a strip of white, as if the ocean had grown a shimmering halo. As the strip moves closer it becomes a devilish moustache.

A dread crown. A wall of fulgent horror. The village is eclipsed by the sea, all souls are surrendered to the outrageous forces inherent in the elements, all memories, all dreams are dissolved, and the body is subjected to dark gravitation for all eternity.

In a ghostly parallel, when I allowed the pains of desire to gather their forces on my own private horizon, I felt my ribcage freeze and collapse—I was starting to suffocate. A wave of want, of need, of desperation arose in my toes and snowballed up my spine and exploded my mind, whose fragments rained back down on my body in confetti of ashes. My lips went hot, my legs vibrated like piano strings, a steel claw of pain fanned out from my coccyx to my perineum. I writhed as if gripped by hunger or disease. I felt my private parts to be singed and tortured into a frenzy. I took armfuls of the sheets and blankets and shoved them between my legs to try and stifle the spreading conflagration. This only made it worse.

Federico had retired to the bathroom, I could see through the door that he was seated naked on a deep marble windowsill, his hands full of smoke and wine and *De Rerum Natura*. My importunate gaze crept across the threshold of his mind. He looked up. I spread myself out on the bed and made a high-pitched noise with my mouth shut. I turned over and raised my behind in the air and waved it about like the crown of a tree swinging in a storm. I shoved my face into the bed as hard as I could. I screamed into the sheets and I gasped for air, I drank it in with great relish and I screamed into the sheets again. And I waited.

TWENTY-ONE

"LISTEN TO YOUR BODY"

"Listen to your body. What does it tell you to do, in this moment, here in this cracked castle of the Palisades, in the year of our Lord . . . in the presence of so many fallen souls, aching and crying to drag you down into their mutual abyss? What do you see down there, in your fouled up imagination, cultivated by so many sufferings at the hands of your family, your teachers, your early romantic follies, your aloof and mysterious elders, your crying siblings, your love partners who just want to bury you inside of them? What do you see as your fate here in this hour, the latest hour you will ever experience, the night, Polonius, the night. Your body, that incomparably small container for your expansive spirit, what is it telling you? What do you want, Polonius? It is all here for your taking."

I lay on my stomach, and Jackie, who weighed no

more than a can of sardines, was sitting on my behind, pulling on my ears and hair, and digging her little thumbs into my neck and shoulders and under my wings. Her voice sounded like that of a songbird whose voice was hoarse from the singing. Her position made it so that our lower orifices communicated with one another, a vaguely unsettling yet congruous sensation. A fair breeze stirred up the many species of sharp sweat present in the room's atmosphere and commingled them with the more intimate bouquets in the lower strata. The breeze also brought the sound of birds, which were beginning to become evening birds.

"I do not see the world in terms of wanting and not wanting. I want—but I want all of this and none of this. I want one of you and the other, and all of you, and I want so many others who are not here—all at once, and none of those desires is diminished by the other. If I were to let my desires go to battle with one another, if I weighed them with an eye to excluding all but the most worthy, if I began a day, or a book for that matter, by holding myself to a particular ending, or a particular evening, I would become that battle, I would never know what my true desire was. I only know my fate by living it. You, for example, I love more than anyone who ever lived. I could also forget about you completely in the next ten minutes—especially if you left, and one of your compatriots took over."

Jackie shifted, but did not so much squirm as deepen her position in the saddle. Her gentle shock of hair crammed against my coccyx.

"But Polonius, if you forget about your eternal intellectualization of things, if you forgot about all those arguments I cannot argue with—for I cannot argue with the general uncertainty of your existence—if you forget even that you had a mind, just listened to your body, what would it say? Would it say?"

"Cigarette."

"Is that all? We will give you a cigarette, and then we will all gather our things to go…"

"No, I mean, cigarette, because I need to think about it."

"Don't think! Be!"

I smoked. Jackie removed herself from me. I turned onto my back, and the other girls began to rise slightly onto their knees and forearms and feet and face me like flowers to the sun.

"There. Now what?"

"Chiara."

Chiara was a Ligurian marine biologist. She had lingered in the woodwork of last night's orgy, uncertain of how to behave. She came to me and, in a risk-free wager as to my intentions, placed her haunches where her head should be.

"Why Chiara?" said Jackie.

"It is evident, on the face of her."

"No, you do not get to cop out. Otherwise it is all for naught."

"Because I want her to feel . . ."

"Not her. You, Polonius. You."

"Because I want to feel her feeling me feeling her. It's a funhouse mirrors situation. A short the mental circuit kind of situation. And I want you to see it happen, because me and you, you and I, are forbidden this experience."

"Who says forbidden? There is no one stopping us. Do you think we came all this way, and assembled this whole indulgence, out of a sense that it was, in the end, forbidden? There is nothing forbidden anymore, Polonius. It is all in your head. All in your head. All in your head. All in your head. How can it be forbidden to give and receive pleasure, if that is indeed what we are doing?"

"It has been, since the beginning of time. There is no measure apart from the human measure. You cannot simply sweep it away, saying, what God or gods will strike me down if I do this thing? I tried that, it leads down the cornhole of nihilism. And the gods do strike, they do strike, just not in the way we are expecting, for that would be too easy to avoid. They withdraw behind the veil of car crashes, train wrecks, conflagrations, terminal disease. Those ills strike in pure random. They also strike in ways that incapacitate the victim from realizing why, or how. Death in a way is too little a punishment. Notice how the cursed in the myths are left alive, just metamorphosed into little wind-up dolls with the plaint of that last suffering on their lips, ever to repeat. The narcissus flower. The birds. The real payback is to stay alive, and to remember. And if you claim to forget, if you claim to be able to forget, you are lying, for the ethereal part of you cannot leave, it never really engaged in the process of arriving. It is made up of all human history folded over itself. And so, I can have the indulgence of this pleasure now, of you watching me do what I am about to do, and knowing that I will have some delight in the reciprocal pain, however later that may be. For the more unbearable the pain, the greater the pleasure was in the first place."

I said all this with Chiara's tan behind poised, patiently, just above my face, so that each breath drew into my nostrils equal parts flora and fauna—the two-headed rose—the fount and infamy of Chiara's existence—the girl's Janus. Chiara's stomach and chest hovered over my body like a quilted pillow of benevolent yet expressive clouds over the earth. Her mouth waited to find its anchor in what she grasped in her hand ever more firmly. We balanced so. The girls balanced too, in what forms and in what relations to each other I could not tell, my eyes were aimed down the barrel of Chiara's being, but I could tell that they, and Jackie, were still.

Jackie made a deep droning sound, like someone being pulled through time against her will. I opened my mouth.

What happened next has been wiped from my memory. I remember only the dream I had when I fell asleep. I was swimming at sea. It was not an irrepressibly stormy situation—I could hear the sea birds plopping into the water around me, and I could hear their cries to one another, a choir of laughter and panic. Here came the sun, diving and flitting about the waves. It spread itself over the surface of the water like an oil slick, and drew itself up and aloof into the heavens like a proper representation of itself. Then it was everywhere like a phosphorescent cloud of mosquitoes, and it was nowhere as if God had gathered up its light and put it in his pocket. I was swimming, and in my dream I was conscious of the act of dreaming and the temptation to interpret. What is interpretation? How do we know when we have reached the thing behind the thing? Does the mere fact of a hard-to-reach location make one thing or conceit more valuable than another? I find, too, that the sinister, the darker, the savage interpretation is the one we land on, as if we are all finding reasons why we ought to cry rather than laugh, or as if truth ought to be sharp like a sword, or explosive like a volatile gas, and do harm. Destruction is safer than creation, one cannot utterly fail at fouling something up. So I thought, swimming, dreaming, conscious of the fact that I would have to interpret my circumstances before the dream spirits took them away from me. I also had realizations about shapes—about the relationship of the triangle to the square to the circle—that are sacred and incommunicable. This was just before—or just after—who can tell time in such a setting, where moments are spread out over years and years over moments—I collided with something, or someone, at a speed and at an angle that must have been perfect, for I instantly exploded. I felt myself come apart—the skull, the innards, the fingers and ribs and all their contents were scattered over the water in a wide shadow like dust swept off the Saharan wastelands and rained down on the castles and canyons of the Atlantic.

With what, or with whom, had I collided? At first I thought it was Jackie, for when I opened my eyes the first sight I saw was of her eyes—bright, hungry, and joyously lascivious. For several hours, as I rolled back the orgies of the past several days and nights, as I herded out all the revelers in a chain of hired cars and bid Jackie to please return alone tomorrow, I labored under the assumption that it was, indeed, her—and that the dream's message was superficially clear. But as I recrossed my threshold after Jackie left, a nausea crowded my brain, and I knew this particular vertigo as the all too familiar feeling of being wrong about something. Jackie was a shaman, a healer, a necromancer maybe, but no destroyer. Was this being not proximate but distant? A vision of November air-mailed in for my dream's bewilderment? This thought made my nausea even more immediate and indiscriminate, and I turned myself upside down and inside out over the toilet.

Outside the bathroom window, the seabirds had lost their minds. They circled, they dove, they doubled themselves over with hilarity and disbelief. I felt that they were laughing at me—an overgrown, overfed, overfucked and overphilosophized monkey who could not sort out the contents of his own mind. A challenge of sorts issued by blind nature. I righted myself, and I went through more paces of purification. I took a cold shower, and I tackled the chaos that my revelers had left behind. All the windows were opened, the air renewed. All the surfaces, the faucets, the levers, the counters, the toilets, the showers, the tubs—received a fresh coat of bleach. I re-catalogued and re-alphabetized my bookshelves—quite a few volumes had been raped and murdered, or left for dead, by my captors and captives. Sheets and towels and blankets and washcloths were piled up and purified. Dishes and utensils I labored over until the skin on my fingers had become clay again. What I did not have the energy to wash, I threw out, and I made many trips laden with grand ballooned black plastic bags into the blinding daylight and down the serpentine driveway to the road and up again, feeling like a lone colonist left behind in a village scourged by a plague. Then I got down on my knees and scrubbed the floors. Inch by inch I extracted the days and nights from where they had fallen. I gathered up dozens of different shapes and breeds and hues of hair. I scraped up patches of body paint, apertif, smashed fruits, fossilized chips, dried blood, and its dirty uncle human excrement. I found eggshells, raisins, capers, bits of smoked meat, cherry stems, lollipop sticks, puddles of Drambuie and Fanghetto and Molinari, shreds and curls of rolling tobacco, a stuffed elephant on a keychain, a tattoo of a cartooned bubble gum wrapper that looked as if it had been burned into the face of the tile. I labored in mellow silence until my domain was bright white again. I walked the halls and rooms until I was satisfied, and I sat down on a couch in an advantageous corner of the living room, from which I could survey the sky, the sea, and the interior spaces in all their sanitary splendor.

I spent the next few hours shaking like a mongrel and staring at a bottle of liquor that stood turgid and unopened in the black rounded mirror of the television, to the right of my own bloated reflection. When the sunlight began to deepen and darken into scarlet, I finally drank. I shivered with delight. The drug helped me retake possession of my body. The candle that had let me believe that my world and my existence were insignificant and therefore free of obligation was slowly snuffed out, and I was once again caged among my walls and very much alone. I did not mind. I drank some more, until the features of my domain began to take on little lives of their own. I could feel, as much as one can feel, the beating heart at the center of my mind. I waited, still, patient. Layer by layer, and without the interference of my volition, the dream was revealed to me again.

I still did not know the face or the name of the being reflected in the sea opposite me just before I was vanquished in the dream, but I could see its features more clearly. The being was not Jackie or November, it was a man. Unlike me, he was gifted with a natural physique. And unlike me, his eyes mirrored the brighter colors of the sea rather than burying them. In a way his eyes were windows straight through his skull to the filmy sky above. He had a long, delicate set of eyelashes that flowed together in the currents and seemed to have a curiosity of their own. In between his eyes was a nose of Huguenot perfection. The cleft of his chin was penciled in but not painted yet. His Adam's apple was barely noticeable against the strong flesh of his neck. The northern yet prosperously hued skin of his body was wrapped tight around his bones and all but hairless. His frame, very much unlike mine, which when mirrored always seemed awash in fluid, rippled and bulged with fine inner strength. He had been born this way—he was a natural athlete, though he had not intentionally exercised a day in his life. The hands and feet were flexed and aware like four miniature bodies outposted at his extremities. At the center of that star, the reproductive parts were well formed and proportionate even in their dormancy, and possessed no more than the dusting of hair you might find on the forearm of a girl.

What was the look on his face? I wish I could sum it up in one word—"Miserable", or "Maudlin, or "Murderous". I wish I could read myself better, for that man swimming at me was part of me, even before I knew him. And I wish I could peel away the layers of what would become the future, and see him for what he was back then, not merely for what he would become. For all of us, the end is certain.

Next morning, Jackie showed up prepared to travel. She drove us out into the mountains, to a villa belonging to one of her boyfriends or girlfriends. The winds were so high that the ground had become carpeted with dust and the leaves and golden needles of autumn. There were garden paths punctuated with ornate wooden benches, fruit trees, a central room with a fireplace large enough for human sacrifice, there were arches that led to sequential identical yet cavernous bedrooms, giving one the sense that the home had been abandoned for centuries by a coterie of sick Franciscans. Everything that happened on the property was hidden from its neighbors by fat pines, primeval arborvitae, and high walls that had been swallowed up by queen's wreath and clematis and lavender. The view was to other mountainsides, a hazy valley, and the sky. Uphill from us, a spring gave birth to a stream that fed a natural stone pool in the center of the garden with water so cold that it could rejuvenate a soul from any state of toxicity or regret. A wine cellar materialized. We sat in the feathery grass. I listened while Jackie recounted her childhood. She had fifty-nine mothers—she had counted them once, she lost count just there, and the number stuck. Her father was one father who came and went a thousand times, each time in a different disguise. Her first sexual encounter was with herself, at age three. She was in a department store with her mother, or one of her mothers. She laid down on a pile of discarded clothes in the dressing room, and she thought of birds flying in a flock, all in tandem and all with a particular twitch to their wings. Her orgasm was remote but beautiful. From then on, she had needed no one and no thing. The fullness that invested her led her to reject many suitors. The first was a boy, the son of one of her mothers. They were seven or eight. Upon Jackie's demurral the boy swallowed a bottle full of antihistamine. The last was a deposed princess from Berlin, with whom Jackie crossed paths in a corner pizzeria in St. Jean Cap Ferrat while her mothers were whoring in the diceways of Monaco. The sunset was warm and pinkish. The wine and tobacco were deep and tannic. The two girls fit together like two halves of a relic found on separate continents. They walked the overgrown paths of the estate abandoned by King Leopold the Belge. They finished and discarded their bottles. They walked through the gates of the princess's villa, four walls of glass that crowned a promontory at the peninsula's southern and most savage point, where the sea could be heard making noise of all hours. Then the princess offered Jackie a lifetime of freedom and indulgence. To which Jackie replied, what freedom I have is not for you to give me. She took a cab to Monaco and spent the night sucking the ridiculously turgid uncircumcised cock of a racecar driver from Madrid, while one of her mothers sucked on the balls. Jackie's sentimental education led her to distrust anyone who claimed to have the beauty, the power, or God forbid the money to hold her interest past the point of satiety. She would never marry.

"I cannot give what I do not own, and my soul belongs to these frantic skies, this dying night, the birds and their hardship of singing and having to sing always again to believe they are heard. I want to sing just once, and for all, but my body, at the moment when I believe it is full of the sound of my own voice, empties again. A lake with no dam is a stream, always yet never present. That is what I feel inside of me always. I feel life flowing into me so strongly through the eyes and the nose and ears, the tactile senses, the memory, the imagination, but with every exhale I lose the philosophical mountains, the sexual dawns, the artistic dreamscapes I try so hard to hold onto. If I could get them all out onto canvases before they turned to craters, sunsets, nightmares—but I cannot paint so quickly, I stand before the easel deathly afraid of what is going to escape me next. It is like eating a beautiful meal, but knowing that the end result will be far less appetizing."

"What about when we fuck . . . "

"When we fuck, you and me you mean?"

"You and me."

"When we fuck, you and me. It is as if we gather all the bad spirits and put them on a ship, like Noah's ark, two of each—guile and vanity, jealousy and self-doubt, laziness and waste, throwing up of one's hands and throwing in of the towel, hopelessness and despair, pretension and dissemblance, anger and prudishness— we herd them all onto Noah's ark and we bid the floods to come, and we set the ship on fire, and we puncture its hull, and we throw giant fish heads out to draw in the sharks. The flaming embers and ashes cascade down on the sea, and then everything is indeed silent for a moment. When we reach orgasm, which for some reason we reach at the same time, the spirits are rejuvenated and we have to go out and gather them again. But I do not mind the chore. . ."

I closed Jackie's mouth with mine. She tore at my lips, she tore at my clothes, she tore at my skin. We fought each other's whims to search for a place to consummate. In one of those monkish rooms, with the desert winds raging through all night, the ashes, the ships, the spirits had their tenuous interplay, just as she had described them. We expired in starfish formation and let the air purify our bodies. I remember waking up in the middle of the night and feeling the sensation that my existence was a vivid dream, that desire and experience, imagination and reality, had finally tied the knot. The sound of Jackie's breathing, the undulation of her belly, the expression of communion and familiarity with the unknown on her sleeping face, the formation of her arms—one out to the side, one across her waist, as if she were about to take a bow—her presence felt at once preordained and impossible. I touched her. She sprung awake. We joined again and expired.

The dream cycle repeated itself until we were, for all intents and purposes, dead in each other's arms.

—

TWENTY-TWO

"DRUGS WERE THE ANSWER"

Drugs were the answer to all my prayers that evening, as I had none of the energy I would have needed to depart my room. The darkness capped the day. A light sense of fumes drifted into my upper windows from the cars that lingered in the narrow street below. They were lined up for the remains of a wedding, I remember now. The bride was a husky little girl, the groom was an androgynous wimp of a fellow. He wore a tuxedo with tails that scratched the ground as he waddled into the waiting car. Guests smoked and checked their watches. The in-laws helped each other take baby steps down the street. Children ran back and forth across the road and clung to their mothers' thighs. Now and then an ancient wind came down into the city canyon and rendered all impressionist. The best man stood aloof with a pile of notecards and rehearsed his speech. What was one to say?

I walked back to the bed and rolled around, to spread Federico's semen into the sheets. The sensation of being unclean shocked me with its indulgence, but it also made me yearn for shelter, for safety, for removal. The monumental curtains were drawn tight. Would that I had noseplugs and earplugs too, I thought, so that my body could be hermetically sealed against the offending elements. The foxholes in my memory. The machine gun fire of my admirers. The diesel fumes of my own secret wants. Rain of inertia. The amputated limbs of the unexpressed. Fog of the imagined thoughts of other people, desert heat of their imagined feelings. The fiery wheel of what they had uttered to me so many years ago, unwitting of how deeply their stylus penetrated this wax tablet. I wished I could plug all the pores of my body to protect me from their eyes.

I rolled myself in blankets, to shelter my psyche from itself. The images began to fade, but as they did, a set of angelic blue eyes, almost white in their innocence, were set off against a deepening black background. Sabbatino—these were his abandoned eyes that watched me circle him on my horse, in a time that felt no more distant than yesterday. As a girl I had no thing, so to speak, for older men—I had no thing for anyone—so I let Sabbatino's affections grow until he could not contain himself any longer. Sabbatino poured his heart out to me one Sunday afternoon, after all the hands had left and my mother and father were at the vet putting down Four Score for his laminitis. Sabbatino cried through his fingers, and his tears stained his chaps black. His confession of love was the most eloquent I ever received. He was not after mere earthly delight . . . the force I possessed was borne of the galaxies and the universe . . . he had no doubt or hesitation . . . he would leave his wife and three children without a thought and without ceremony . . . he would wait until I was of proper age, and seek my parent's premeditated consent . . . . Unfortunately, as the elegant Sabbatino wept, all I could see was his future: the taut sunlicked skin of his sagelike face stretched to a frame twice his size then reapplied to his body. Permanent offal gathered at the corners of his lips. Deflated breasts punctuated by thick knobby nipples hung over a bald, alcoholic belly . . . . He would give me shelter and security for the rest of my life, he would take me back to Chile, where we could live in the protection of towering mountains, and no one and no thing could touch us or give us reason to want. At such altitude, the weather was fair and perfect. And when we wanted to escape further, we could make our way to Las Gaviotas, or to his family cabin at the end of the world on Lago Los Molinos, but all I could think about was his bloated body, ruddy and hairless and covered in moles, and my still-blooming soul debased by the act of wiping his flabby, water-filled ass, or hosing him off like a monstrous infant in the bathtub. I threw up all over Sabbatino's boots, and kindly asked him to leave and never return. The words he uttered next, I believe, were the last words that Sabbatino ever spoke to me before committing himself to a Franciscan monastery, somewhere in the hills or mountains or plateaus between the Sierras de Cordoba and Valparaiso. They were the gentlest words he could have used, but gentle words are the profoundest poison to a girl that does not want to hear them.

"I will do as you wish, and I will live out the remainder of my life in waiting for you to return to me, just as the mendicant awaits the return of Christ."

Sabbatino went to the monastery of Franciscan monks at Santo Spirito de Mano de Jesus de Maria Cristobal y Eugenia. I wrote him many letters, which were never answered and never returned. Then I started writing him letters and never sending them, instead I hid them in my copy of Lombardo's *Iliad*, where they still sleep, my maimed messengers of an amorous apocalypse. I have tried to read them, but they are incomprehensible to me. They are so alive with emotion that their reality cannot be parsed. When I read them, my brain starts swimming in wax. For it seems that I have loved that absent monk more than I have loved any real person. Sabbatino was everything I wanted him to be, especially when I was asleep and dreaming, and alone.

He was alive in my dreams, he showed up cloaked in the epithelium of his soul. All agape with smiles, his teeth shone like newborn stars. The darkness around us shone phosphorescent. The wet streets were grit, regret, humanity. His eyes these moonlike marbles. Everything forgiven. There is nothing so divine as everything forgiven. For it is humanly impossible to forgive everything.

I fell into his arms and a state of perpetual . . .

This was the point at which he would dissolve and I would awaken, my body a hot coal that could not sleep again for days. I would wander out into the moonlight like a gypsy. Shaking hands, belly hungry and would not fill when fed. I would tear at my hair, a cartoon maniac, and I would chase the night fog all the way to the horizon, hoping that it would hide me and shelter me. The fog consistently declared it was not made as a blanket for the damned, and it retreated several hundred paces towards the wood line. I would chase it again, into the forest and its sculpted world of stuffed birds and angels. The forest closest to my childhood home was a series of miniature ravines, and in each ravine a stream guarded by pines and beeches and the occasional screaming white birch. The miniature ridgelines shading these streambeds were like the tombs of whole armies buried where they fell. If I followed the run of a stream until I lost sight of the clearing behind me, I entered a world entirely without compass, and I was finally calm.

In such silence of mind, I made the resolutions that formed my life. They were all unspoken, blood flows and tectonic rises and shivers of the soil that no one can explain. I would never again deny myself love. The pain of knowing that Sabbatino languished in the far reaches of Patagonia, alone but for the gilded icons of a death cult—and that my hand had driven a cold dagger into that heart and broken it off at the handle—was too much for me to bear. My own heart was broken inside his chest. It was done.

The immediate result for that fourteen year-old girl who decided to embrace her sex was a great deal of sport-fucking, the annals of which could fill volumes. I had a youth full of sport-fucking, stolen from every moment the night brought silence down on the earth. Then I took a gap year in Montevideo, and I dried out. On a break for Semana Santa, I took a flight to Valparaiso and set out from the airport in a screwloose Mitsubishi with a map and a bottle of Cutty Sark. At dawn, in the cloister of Santo Spirito de Mano de Jesus de Maria Cristobal y Eugenia, I found Sabbatino. I spent five days with him at the Montpelier mountain lodge just outside of the village. This was not sport-fucking but the ecstasy of immortality. And as punishment for his greedy foretaste of the afterlife, Sabbatino was summarily defrocked. Now Sabbatino runs a small mechanic's shop on the Via Aurelia on the way out of Vatican City. His new wife is a drily humored white feathered Italian girl named Saira. Last time I saw him, on my way from Calabria to Milan, he was tending his artichokes and picking larvae off his hothouse tomatoes in a state of unquantifiable bliss.

The difference with Turner, I reflected as I listened down the hall for Federico's snoring and flew down my back staircase to the alleyway and out into the sweltering Philadelphia night, was that happiness, writ however one may choose to write it, was entirely out of the question. Desire merged with suffering unto death—I had not yet experienced the two stirred together in such an undifferentiated cocktail. In quick succession yes. As when I found that my Shakespeare professor, a man whose name and reputation I will keep safely locked away, had a faulty heart valve and could not make love standing up lest he lose consciousness. Or when one of my horses was euthanized at the mouth of my father's revolver and hoisted onto the back of a flatbed truck to be processed for dog feed. Or when Polonius flew off to California for his sabbatical, and I trashed the car all the way home, I inadvertently sounded the horn a thousand times at so many innocent passers-by, knowing that his absence would throw me into the inferno of psychosis in which I still burned. The difference with Turner was, that the ecstasy and the inferno were so closely interwoven that they did not deserve to be assigned to two different words.

Down by seventh or eighth street I stopped walking. If I could have, I would have dropped to the pavement and become a work of human graffiti. I had not eaten since the night before. I peeked into a few cafes. I could not join any of the people there. I kept moving. How different the world was from the one I had imagined. It was not the fault of the people, it was not the fault of the city, it was not the fault of the frazzled beggars or the spent women. The world had invented its colors long ago—the treasured blue on white, sometimes dissolving into a sonorous effervescence—the gold on green of the rising sun—and the black on black where I now lived, where no message or import was distinguishable from the night. There was a time in my life when such an environment would have felt natural, even reassuring—back when there was such a thing as a choice.

I reached for the laden brass stirrup that adorned Turner's front door.

Where do I begin?

It was dark, dark, dark, too dark to be real. An ambient moonlight, although there was no moon and no light, half illuminated the foyer and an anteroom where a mantis-like figure played the piano. She nodded at me, and she swam her eyes upward against her weighty and roseate eyelids.

I climbed the stairs. On the first landing there shivered the fingers of a ridiculous bassist. He did not seem to know where to put them, yet his instrument seemed to know which notes to play. Certain strings rang out without his bidding or blessing. His body roiled and ricocheted against the air. The head of the bass was missing all but one tuner knob. The head of the man was missing all but three or four teeth. A cigarette dangled from his lip with nothing to hold it there. I kept climbing.

I heard Turner long before I saw him or knew where he was. His saxophone spoke to me. It told me I was a moth-winged creature and my life would be spent circling a light I would never know—whether star, mirror, or electric charge caged in a glass. Then the music disappeared, it went underground in my bones, and I saw him.

Before that night, like many dramatic purists of my kind, I had been a knee-jerk hater of the device known as the *deus ex machina*. I had not realized there was a deus and a machina inside of me, which I loosely translate as, the machine of the impossible.

I crawled up to Turner and I debased myself at his feet. I curled my arms around his ankles and rested my head on his shoes and shed tears. I begged him for forgiveness for all my sins, as if I had arrived at Jerusalem from Malaga with ten thousand children in tow and had witnessed them disemboweled one by one by my own folly. What I had done or not done, or how I might have exercised more control or volition over my actions was not clear. The not knowing him before—the not having found him or listened to his entreaties, in so many different forms—the wasting of so much time in hesitation—my blindness—all was blashpemy.

Love is a dirty word, and this was not love for me anyhow, it was...

I was Athena shoved back into the head of Zeus—I was swimming in it—it was all over me—too close to me for me to know what it was—and the albumen of Zeus' brain was too thick for me to see through. I could hear, however, with splendid clarity. The underwater voices spoke of armies, of naiads, of feasts, of famines— of the future misery of keels still under the shipbuild- er's final touches—to be launched and scattered and scuttled in still unknown waters—of a rooftop scene in technicolor—of the hands of a woman and their myr- iad snaking creases stung by nettle at the riverbank— of the catalogue of morning sounds, of the sky's pain at being split in two by the sun's fire—of the poison of Zeus' bloody feud with Saturn, that consumed all but a modicum of his creative energies, which modicum fueled all the world's dramas—of his time spent playing in different forms, where his wife would not find him—visions of existing as a field of grass given in to the cleansing breeze, and visited by his best friends, who peopled his breast with flower heads.

The underwater voices spoke of the world's reality as an infinite set of reflections, and the scale of things as a matter merely of the angle and curvature of the mirror in question. But such an insight did not diminish the immortality of our souls or the depth of the trenches under the oceans or the serenity of the river Styx or the eternity of our rotations or the shine of a watery eye. The voices spoke of how, when I rested my head in the cradle of Turner's feet, the absence of pain was all I could ever hope for—spoke of the one way to get there short of decapitation.

I walked my fingers up along the backs of Turner's ankles and I cupped them around his thighs. He touched my head—as lightly as you would a newborn's—and the circle was complete.

—

TWENTY-THREE

"THE ANIMATION OF THE BODY SPIRIT"

"The animation of the body spirit takes practice, Polonius—but not in the way you would predict—and not in a way that is repeatable. Because the tides and salts of the body-spirit live by the rotations of their own moons—and these were set in motion long before our births.

"Not repeatable...

"We spend the lion's share, even more, we spend the plupart, the best part of our energies, fearing who we might be. I do not say fearing who we are in fact, because that cannot be known. Such as I—such as I—existed long before I knew you. But then you merged into me, and I am unrecognizable to myself. I do not know the person who used to inhabit my body—if we are even people after all. If we are not in fact individuals, then this life begins to make sense to me—as a melody played on so many levels—from F sharp minor to Karakoram. And we are collections of notes with certain and uncertain timbres. Not species at all but collections of voices from a choir.

"I am now inundated with you. We are not separable even though we might awaken tomorrow in a different dream, in a different life. We define ourselves in terms of the scant memories we have of our reflections in the landscapes of the past. Our actual reflections in this painted glass are as impermanent as the flies of Aristophanes.

"The real substance in life comes when a man sees an upside-down spruce forest in a lake—a blue eye of the earth—and dislodged from it like a zygote the turgid insomniac moon. And he recognizes his face in nature, just as I recognize my face in yours, Polonius. The symmetry in your expressions—faith and despair—withdrawal and fulfillment—motion and stillness mixed— you and I—who and who—what and what—there is no way to tell—nature gives us no clues to distinguish two minds—two spirits—two souls—from each other. You and the spruce. Who is to say that the one is not the other, and that your pain is not the pain of that being, made to stand so still in the moonlight—in another dimension? The austere, the rational, call such thoughts frivolous— but the life of the mind is really none of their business.

Those who denigrate the imagination will never make any contribution to the field of thought.

"Imagine a lightning bug squinting at the sun, thinking, it must be impossible because I cannot seem to do it. We do not have a yardstick long enough to measure the breadth of the universe, and still we doubt the presence of the divine here on earth—here where, under this paper-thin blanket of atmosphere, we inhabit a ribbon of green between us and nowhere.

"The patently impossible is true—so who is to say that I have not disappeared—that my body is not merely a mirage—and that now you carry me inside of you—a man pregnant with a girl.

"And in turn, how many times have you disappeared inside of me, Polonius? We must needs consider our origins, if our forbears were similarly nested inside each other like Russian dolls. Or was the metaphor of their existence entirely different? Were they the threads of this cushion, discrete yet indistinguishable from one another? Were they the oil of a masterpiece over which time has jessoed—and are we the salt air that wears away the layers back to the beginning?

"How is it that you put yourself inside of me and it feels you are replacing something that was stolen from me, long before I knew you. Or to collapse time, are you giving me a foretaste, merely, of what I am going to lose when I am dead? And is it this that drives me mad."

Jackie rested from speech. She buried herself in the sensation of the fine evening air against her body. We lay on stone benches beside a black swimming pool full of sycamore leaves. The breeze picked up the hairs on our bellies and harvested tears from our eyes. The necks of wine bottles howled at pitches according to their degrees of fullness. I looked at my hand.

The only thing left is revolution, I thought.

I looked at my hand again. The proportions of the fingers to one another were foreign to me, as if I'd dropped out of space. I curled the fingers, and the nails stared back at me like five sickly eyes. They knew something I did not—they made up a foreign precinct of my evolution—a time when I had clung for dear life to the branches of strangler vines against the lure of impact with the forest floor. My legs too seemed cut from the cloth of another creature, a herd animal who had need of such meat for walking long distances to find water over parched savanna. In the middle of this the cock, which struck me as all too human, stared up at me with vanquished incredulity. Why all the abuse, it asked, all the while nodding and seeming to acknowledge the ingratitude of its question—or any question assuming surfeit of the statue lying next to me, the miracle of anthropomorphic art. Jacqueline Cerny.

Candles revealed and occluded her. Her stomach rippled with her breathing, her nipples, vigilant, from among strands of her black hair unwashed for so many days, took stock of the night sky. Her skin swung from a ghostly pale to a fiery sunburst to the vanishing hues of her background, an olive tree that resembled a perfectly formed cloudlet of hummingbirds. My body felt her so closely it boiled over. Parts of me were left in the cracks between the paving stones. I pooled into a reservoir, I bubbled into the ground, I evaporated and coalesced with the sweat of the night. Then "I", fire condensed as rain, fell back down in fragments to where I lay.

I looked at Jackie again, and the compound weight— and weightlessness—of ecstasy took hold of me once more.

I wish there existed a language, whose sole purpose was to describe the feeling that inhabited me that night. Imagine a sailboat of some weight, the mast reaching far into the sky—the boom as thick as an arm of the cyclopes. It is sailing along, this boat, when the sailor spots a speck of rust on the horizon. He ignores it, and tends to the curvature and the cleanliness of his own dominion. He reckons the weather, sets his course, and drops down into his cabin for a smoke and a light nap.

He dreams of a house with porous walls, he can hear the trajectory of history through them. Piles of Mayans are burning. The Blitz is on. The great divide of time and space is rising through the center. People are being separated from themselves. His mother is near. She is not worried, she is even as calm as a sleeping limb—alive yet absent—and the louder the sailor screams, the less his mother seems to care. Didn't you know, son, didn't you know, this was bound to happen? And a certainty should not cause your brains to scramble themselves in such a fashion. You are a grown man, for one...

He opens his eyes. There is no one around. He feels nonetheless a presence.

The room darkens as if by the shade of a storm. Ah—the romance of the rain, whispers the sailor, and he drifts back to sleep. He awakens—years or moments later he has no idea—on the floor of his cabin and rolling towards the door. There is a scream coming from above the hatchway—it is his boat. The sheets are cracking. The sails ripple and smack their cheeks. The sailor's library flies off its shelves and pelts him with the dead weight of Philosophy. He crawls on the walls towards the darkness of day. He slips down the deck towards the gunwale, and he catches a glimpse of what has befallen his boat. The sea is the sky and the sky is the sea. He feels the keel breach the surface. A whole landscape of field and intermediate forests of water looms above his head. In a final act of not so much self-preservation as the desire to have a final act, he grabs the wheel with one hand and with the other makes the sign of a cross. He is engulfed.

When the trusted sailboat rights itself and the sailor sweeps the matted hair back from his face, he sees receding from him that speck of rust, now a ship the size of a city and as tall as a city's highest spire. From its stern flies every flag imaginable, and it is moving at a ridiculous pace. Its wake sends storm surges for miles, as if by the impact of a meteor. The sailor goes about taking stock of his belongings and the state of his boat, when he realizes, on his knees in a sordid heap among the offal of his journey, that he has, at some point during the subconscious impact of his body and the force of nature thrown off by that ghost ship, surrendered to a secret climax.

He rigs his keel as efficiently as his bloodied hands will allow, and he plots a course to head off that ghost ship at its next logical port of call. In hopes, in dreams, of being engulfed again.

Every metaphor has its breaking point—where it fails to illustrate—where it runs out of ink. Jackie shattered her comparisons when she—as she did now—reached out and touched me. With the other hand she took a deep guzzle of a bottle and passed it to me. She climbed on my chest and tilted the bottle upside down until it gurgled its last in my throat. What came to me was brain damage—brain damage so sweet, so rare, so voluptuous, so indulgent, so lucid, so autumnal, so pungent, so weighty, so elevating—the brain damage damaged that part of my brain that was grounded to the affairs of the small, the riddling masses, the disgraced, the flailing charlatans peddling their wares to a vapid god—it damaged all the parts of me I despised—I would have drowned myself, just to drown those parts. Yet here they were banished from my consciousness, leaving not even the imprint of their absence—simply banished—and the rest was full of Jackie's peculiar version of joy. She took my hand again and placed it on her skin. Words were exchanged, I remember none of them. What I remember, every day of this expiring life, is the sound of her voice and the nature of the space inside of her. We cried out into the night and the sound of each other's voices lifted us up granite cliffs and dropped us from incalculable heights into each other's mouths. I opened my eyes and the sight of the union of our bodies blew me to pieces.

I awoke some time just before dawn. I could feel the air just begin to take on a charge. The birds were making some anticipatory forays into song. I reached for Jackie and pulled her close to me. Her body was drenched in cold sweat, she was shivering so hard that the clamor of her teeth berated my ear. She was moaning a moan in the back of her throat that sounded like the involuntary eructation of a deaf mute or someone who was being burned or tortured. I lost consciousness bereaved, finally, of my thoughts.

I return to that moment as the first, and quite possibly the only, moment in my life when I forgot that Anna Delancey was dead.

No, I am lying. I have never forgotten Anna Delancey's death. In order to forget Anna Delancey's death, I would have had to forget that she ever lived. And to forget her was to forget myself. We are one and the same. All my life I have chased her down the ice curtained desert of that street and sifted for her in the black folds of the river. This has been my destiny, to be a necromancer, to bring into the light what dwells in the dark, to chase after fallen spirits.

I have not spent more than the time it took me to freefall from the bridge, in wondering why Anna Delancey took her life. I always understood that there was no why in this world, there were no reasons. And even if they did exist, if you could string one human impulse after another definitively, like two musical notes always played together in a sequence, you could never capture the precursor to human suicide. At barely twenty years of age, her baby fat still faithfully protecting her hips against the concrete of the library floor, Anna Delancey, her limbs wrapped around the dream of her childhood, had reached the height of her existence. There was no why: she knew. And it was not within my power that night to steal her knowledge away.

I too, enclosed and made cryptic to all but her by her embrace, mouth to mouth with her breathing, had found the end. So why go further, why continue when the best my hands could do was to reenact their caress of her back upon Jackie's, to foretell the fact that everything they held dear would be torn from them after all—had been torn from them already?

There are no reasons known to man. There are the rotations of the earth and the risings and the fallings of the light. That light illuminated Jackie's face, and I gave it a worshipful palm in which to cradle itself. Bastard child of a stripper or no, a touch too serious or a touch too ridiculous, reflection of my insatiate taste for sin, and young, some would say too young, though she was, Jackie was alive.

—

TWENTY-FOUR

"WHAT IS A MAN, AND OPPOSED TO WHAT"

What is a man, and as opposed to what? But first what is a man as opposed to a woman, because those are two categories that supposedly exist. Opposed to anything else approaching a wild animal or beast, a man is a woman. So let us consider what sets him apart from his partner.

We all begin as girls, with boys inside of us—in our futures. Then, some of us become boys with girls inside of us—in our pasts. The yearning for another of the opposite sex is very much a yearning for ourselves.

Before Turner, I knew man in a certain way. My father was a worker, a quiet, benign, meditative worker, much like the honey bee. He took care of the fields and the animals, he listened to my mother, and he listened to me, he gave us an open canvas on which to live. He was never stern, yet he was not one to reveal what was in his heart. Similarly, Polonius was his own sort of monk…a warrior monk perhaps, but still very much a mendicant in his emotions. He expressed himself in the manly silence of his bearing and in the silence of the page, where he tried to map the subterranean rivers of Philosophy. He taught his classes not as a master but as if he were just another student, just another pilgrim at the shrine of his own masters. He never did elevate himself to any level, he did not cry out for attention or recognition.

Nor did I see Polonius even weep when he lost Anna Delancey. Perhaps he did weep. Not with pathos, not out of weakness, but out of self-hatred at his inability to save her, which was quickly stifled by his knowledge that self-hatred was the worst sort of overindulgence. Just the sight, or the concrete thought, of his pain in losing his childhood in such a way made me explode with sadness, so that many times, in those early days by Polonius' side when I sheltered him from jumping in the river again and freezing himself to death, I thought I would regurgitate the contents of my entire body cavity out onto the floor. Meantime he did find laughter, and he did find ways to communicate to me the vast stores of care and tenderness he had stashed away for the nourishment of Anna's body and soul. He did not waste time, or he did not take what he would have called wasted time, in reaching for alternate worlds. He was here, he still is here, to give a certain gift and not another. And he is not overly concerned with what he receives in return. He simply wants the opportunity to make the offering.

Whereas I . . . I have spent the mass of my time on this earth searching for another planet. The girl in me is lost. She needs an anchor, even if that anchor is wreck, ruin, and she thrashes about in the vortex left by the ship for a single sinker to weigh her down. In her hilariously hairless skin she is too naked, and if she is left out in the world alone for more than a few terrifying moments, she will freeze.

And yet the man. The man in his silence, he too needs to be needed. Without a recipient for his offering, he cries out to the world, a broken angel. He is a god who has need of worship, the dance of candlelight, the smoke of incense, the blood of human sacrifice, the doomed exertions of war, the face of a gold coin emblazoned with his death mask.

I remember this circle of thought closing in on me as I, naked, approached the naked Turner and looked him from the bronze static atop his head to his lightly spotted feet. His chest and stomach were so hairy, it would have been impossible for the gods to carve him in stone or clay without using some sort of seaweed to give the accents. He was powerful. His skin was taut. His legs were two casks that constantly intersected with each other, there was no space, really, for his pomegranate balls to dwell between them. There was this presentation of a weapon. All the manhood inside Turner had concentrated in his manhood.

I did what I did. A hundred, a thousand times. When I was with him there was barely time to breathe, I was fucked with deadbolt solemnity. You see my legs were forced apart. My knees were bowed outwards, to make way. The thing came into me like an entire civilization of emotion. And so. Potent, like a drink you have not tasted before and it makes all other drinks taste like water. I have no need of coherence because this period, which lasted I have no sensation of how long, was not coherent. I touched that thing, and my persona was plunged into chaos.

The thing would not fit into my mouth, so I would turn around and put it inside of me the other way. The thing would not fit into me the other way so I would turn around and so on, and so on. The next university term began. We ceded our lead roles in the term's production (I think it was *Midsummer*) to others, there was no time to practice or rehearse, all fictions were meaningless, I had this thing, it was alive, and it shot out all the lights in my heart. In the resultant darkness and silence we lay together and recited each other's histories. My eyes traced the desert landscapes of moonlight

plaster on the ceiling. He spoke. And he gave me eloquence that was strong enough to poison my soul. I
cannot reproduce his style, it was too rich and full of
forms and turns you would not understand, but I can
try to reproduce the substance. I am piecing together a
narrative that I received over so many days and nights,
but they all bleed together now, I see them and feel
them as one image and song. He began,

"I know beyond knowing, I feel beyond feeling, that
I will spend the rest of my life by your side. So I want to
tell you the whole story from the beginning.

"I learned to play music, to summon the spirits
to me when I was very young. I was an only child, I
needed two voices in me—one to entertain the other,
and the other to provide encouragement and approbation to the one. My father is an historian of China. My
mother is an anthropologist specializing in the mys-
ticisms of the Eskimos. But she is also the daughter
of Henry Snead, who invented some kind of industrial brake that is used in everything from the wood-
chipper to the steamship. He died young from overindulgence, from the evidence I have I feel that his
only real goal was to drink himself down under, he
must have been ignored or destroyed spiritually as a
child, and there was no coming back. Unlike her sisters, my mother tolerated Henry's addictions—and
the temperament that accompanied them—and even

encouraged them—he was not an interesting man sober—he was agitated and obsessive and cruel—and she likely poured the drink that killed him. Late in life Henry had disinherited everyone except my mother. After a couple of years moving through the courts and settling out the many claims on Henry's property, we lived a life of unspeakable excess. Although we were situated in Manhattan during the school year, as they both still taught at Columbia, my parents took me around the world each summer, and every time to more remote and even unnamed locales. On one otherwise nondescript sunny afternoon, I was sitting in the Pantheon, a building so often overlooked and undervalued, when the voice of Jupiter spoke to me through that incredible oculus in the roof. He seemed to tell me—I did not understand Latin at the time but I could feel what there was to be felt in the stresses and stops—he seemed to tell me that we were all actors, so the most honest way to make a living was by admitting the truth, and engaging in a lifelong mirage for the entertainment of the people. He also seemed to tell me that his presence could easily be summoned by the right sequence of notes, played on an instrument of one's choice. I said "Yes", and my identity was forged. I was thirteen.

"What began as a benign meditation on the *mirabilis Romae* led me down a path of . . . how shall I say this . . . I became the owner of the two most sensual instruments on the planet, the tenor saxophone and the Telecaster. I wrote two long epic poems no one would ever read, I wrote over a thousand lyrics, each one more imitative than the last. I purchased every meaningful volume in the English language, translated or no, and by the time I was seventeen I read through all of them. I memorized *The Ring and the Book.* I tried writing operas, and found my pen was empty. I contemplated suicide. My mother, who must have felt that my mania was reaching a breaking point, handed me the *Iliad* and told me there was nothing more worthwhile in the world than beginning at the beginning. Over the next six months I made a stack of 12,000 note cards representing every word of Ancient Greek. I knew them backwards and forwards, and soon I was entirely unfit for the world. During the year between high school and college I visited eighty countries. On my travels down through the deserts of Mexico and while camped out with strangers and persistent diarrhea at little dollar-a-night hostels, I soaked up the Romance languages and branched into Japanese and Sanskrit, German and Russian and Czech, and some elementary Indo European. I accumulated whole suitcases full of dictionaries, and when I had decided I had memorized my fill, I got it in my head to lighten my load. I had a little ceremony for my books at the beach way down the isthmus of Central America in Bocas del Toro and set them all on fire. From the steel moonlit ocean and among the company of millions of phosphorescent organisms I watched them burn, and the French girl I was with, a comical and histrionic sort, cried for them and her face was caked in sand from her groveling. She made as if to throw herself on the flames and was rescued, in a way, by a native who somewhat swept her off her feet by his delightful renditions of Chan Chan and Paloma and other folk songs which he played on vinyl strings with an admirable picking style that I still cannot imitate. That night, in the native's open-air bungalow guarded by immense Rottweilers, we skewered my French girl from both sides, and the native introduced me to the delights of cocaine.

"His timing was right. I knew too much. I needed to unknow everything and start again, with the simple sensation of the experience of being alive. When I say that the native's coca powder was pure, I mean it was so pure you could feed it to a baby. I snorted a mountain up my nose during my weeks marooned at the end of the line near the impenetrable forests of La Amistad. It was sufficient to turn my life on its head. There was an entire universe that existed apart from the world of thought I had embraced as a child. I decided to wrap my arms around it and not let go until I had found the source of all this feeling. 'Always do half a line, never a whole line', the native instructed me. 'Otherwise your whole life will change'. His hands shook in that moment, he had not obeyed his own advice. I did not obey him either.

"In the mountains of Peru and Ecuador, in Colombia, in the haunts and the maniac nights of Cartagena I was a king. On the tributaries of the Amazonas I was a prince. On the pampas of Argentina I was a viceroy. On the beaches of Rio de Janeiro I was an aristocrat. On a sailboat through the doldrums to the isle of Tahiti I was a dilletante. When I reached the whore huts of Thailand I was still a playboy, a night chaser, a sports-man. As I worked my way up the coast of China I was a naturalist, an explorer, a scholar. I absorbed my final language, the language of Lao Tsu and the Tao Te Ching, from a set of forbidden flashcards sold to me by a cobbler in Shenyang. I walked whole mountains of the wall, and on the ten-day trip from Harbin to Moscow on the Trans-Siberian I was down to only three or four bumps a day and the blackest of the black Russian teas. When I reached Moscow and wandered the cobbled streets of the Lubyanka, I was still a poet. I translated Khodoseevich's *Smolenskiy Rinok* in a concrete basement bar over a *pol-litra* of vodka and perhaps only a sniff or two in the bathroom from a skeleton key I had har-vested from a riverboat cabin door on the Magdalena. I took myself outside in the black morning and the cold struck me alive in ways that no note of music or sunshine or dream had done on my entire spirit quest from meridian to meridian. The cold made me say to the lords of nature, if you spare me, if you keep me alive through this one phase of harm, I will worship you forever, whoever you are, whatever you are doing up there in that dread palace in the sky. Spare me for one year or many, I don't care, just let me see my way out of this obsession with self-intoxication, this search for a deeper vortex in which to cast my mind. I want to be whole again.

"And the lords of nature did spare me, that night. I walked the glorious boulevards and the variegated back streets of Moscow until the worker bees woke up and started their honest locutions in the shops, in the government buildings, in the buses and tramways. They spared me all the way to the border with Belorussia and my walks through the battlefields of such massacres and regenerations as no one has seen or can imagine. They spared me on an overnight bus ride to Berlin, where I made friends with an old Polish woman who told me the entire history of humankind. When I arrived in Western Europe I became an historian of all such untold histories, and I wore that cloak proudly and patiently and with few words all the way down through the Bernese Oberland and into the foggy plains of Italy. I wore it along the sleepy Riviera and through the wind whipped mountains of Provence and into the Costa Brava and down along the half-naked and sun scorched coast of Spain to the livid streets of Barcelona. I was quiet, I listened—to the girls and their hopeless prattle, to the men and their blandishments and their showy turns of phrase describing curves, trajectories, sunsets, to the sounds of restlessness in the close built squares and the feeling of a Bourbon openness in the parks. I wore it down the coast to Sevilla where I became somewhat enamored with an older woman named Elaine who was close to a masters in horticulture at the Institute. With her I only had a bit of a sip, let us say, at breakfast to cleanse my system and get the cobwebs out, then I was primed for a day of keen and close observation at her studied side, of all the forms of flower and grandiose living organism on those dusty streets.

Somehow I ended up in Amsterdam, a gloomy place which I entirely ignored, and from there I returned to a place I was supposed to call home. Compared to all the places I had seen in my travels, New York City was the most dismal, the most nihilistic, the most fallen, the most vacant, the most senile and wasted and ugly and wretched and self-flagellating, the most god-forsaken place on earth. I gave up my seat at Columbia and enrolled here, not so much out of a taste for particular town but out of protest, and a desire to live apart from all sort of meaningless madness. But I had a week to kill at home, and my parents were away.

"I was alone, in their townhome nearly fronting on the Guggenheim, and did not want to do anything—did not want to fuck, did not want to eat, did not want to drink, did not want to talk, did not want to buy anything or build anything or destroy anything—did not want to do anything except perhaps commit suicide or get a mountain of cocaine and snort it up my nose and hopefully straight into my brain. So I called one of so many phone numbers you used to be able to find right there in the phonebook, and I received a molehill of the purest most sanctified ingredient you could have pulverized out of a cloud of fluff. And I sucked it up my nose first in little bumplets and then in well organized defiles straight as the scratches left on trees from bear's claws and then just in lumps and heaves and rhinoceros doses. I wanted to sleep but could not sleep so I cried all night out of nostalgia for all I had gained and lost on that journey where I had found myself in so many stages of enlightenment. Out in the world, I was an explorer, a prophet, an immortal. In New York, in America, I am a slave.

"My intoxication has rendered me dyslexic. When you hear me recite the voice of Othello it is not from recent practice but pulling from the archives of when I was a younger man and memorized everything. I am walking into the orchard of my mind and harvesting the fruits, which will soon turn sour and go to seed."

As he spoke, over those many days and weeks that are as waves on the Black Sea that monument our exile from one another, I molded my mind to him in the same way as he had embraced his addiction. And on that final night, when he brought his story up to the present and stopped, I molded my body to him and I felt time fold back on itself.

People speak of one's childhood as something to be gotten over, to be conquered, to be understood then discarded. But I say the best version of us is the one that touches ourselves in the beginning. To drink from Turner's body was to taste the milk from my mother's breast. I saw her as she was at my age—rosy, plump, immaculate. Young. She was so young. She was so young her face was as smooth as porcelain even when she smiled or frowned, there were no creases worn on her expression. And she and Turner had each other's bodies in my soul, when he embraced me. The warmth he gave me was as elemental, as necessary as the warmth given to me as a newborn, and once the equation was made I was there, I was complete, there was nothing else to be done in life, you could have lopped off my head and the rest of me merely would have shrugged and crawled its way into the eternal warmth of the grave.

A detail is worth mention, before I descend further down the ladder of my memory. How had I responded to Turner's rabid, indefatigable devotion to cocaine? I fought him, I tried to beat it out of him. Beat the slavery out of him. Beat it, meaning I would see him monstrously high and unable to pick up his instrument and unable to elucidate what he was thinking and unable to carry out conversation, and I would clock him across the face with a closed fist. It was against my nature at first, but the more I did it the more I realized that nothing was against my nature. I tried to beat the addiction out of him, and he did not resist. He just sat there and took the blows, like a dissident who knew the price of his cause. The expression that worked its way into his features over those last weeks was one of stone-cold metaphysical resilience. He was who he was. He took my blows and assembled flutes, dung hills, molehills, rifts, Raritans, Missouris, Santa Anas, Purissimas, Appenines, and finally Alpes of cocaine. And in riveting gargoyle gestures he thrust everything into his brain.

The music died down. I molded my body to him, and he poured into me the roots of my existence. As we lay in the moonlight, his pianist, that wraith with her particular beauty, those delicate daubs of blue that punctuated her scarlet smile, she came into the room and sat with her legs crossed on the carpet and lit a candle and started chanting a prayer. When she was done she stood up and descended the stairs to the parlor, where I could hear her strike up a tune on the grand piano with a melody and a theme congruent with the one I had first heard that rainy, dismal, desperate night I had first sought out Turner. Next came in the bassist with his teeth glowing like jellyfish in the inky maze of his head, his wild fingers bounced against one another with expectant agitation. He bowed, and he descended to the landing and he plucked his upright base and made it send deep vibrations through the structure of my dreams. I drifted off again, in a perfect ecstasy that reached out to the furthest extremities of my body. Everything relaxed, and the body embraced its liquid form.

When I woke up, the pianist was at the foot of the bed again. It was midday. She was convulsing and suffocating herself with sadness. Tears were pooled up on the floor in front of her, so deep that a whole flock of starlings could have bathed in them.

"What is wrong?" I said.

"No no no no no no no no no no no no no," she said.

I rustled in my bedsheets and made as if to redouble their cover of me. I felt very cold. She sprang up and took hold of my body and squeezed with all her might. I tried to awaken Turner with a touch of my foot, but it struck something else, a barrier between me and him, a wall. I made as if to turn, and the girl with all her power dragged me out of bed and onto the floor, and she, bless the pianist, she pushed me out of the room before I could get a glimpse of what was left behind.

TWENTY-FIVE

"WE AWOKE IN THE CLOUDLESS AIR OF FALL"

We awoke in the cloudless air of fall. The trees had little pearls hanging from their fingernails. The light in the air was so plentiful and crisp that it did not know what to do with itself. I rose, and Jackie murmured and starfished on her belly and went back to sleep. I walked naked down the arched breezeway and into the kitchen and made myself an espresso. A halo began to form around me. I went into a farflung bathroom and ran the shower and had a nauseating sort of relief until I was emptied of the hundred glasses of wine and the hundred oysters we had eaten the night before.

In the shower, I took stock of my body. The exoskeleton spoke of a linear progression towards chaos, disintegration, metamorphosis, and banishment. Under the skin, however, was a tree of pleasure stretching its tendrils all the way up to the eggshell heavens. I was looming and indestructible. I touched my body any-where, or I focused on a wrinkle in the clay tile, and my soul went down to a well, an aquifer of pleasure and harvested me a bucket's worth that was just as soon replenished tenfold by its spring. There was a perma-nence to all this—or there was an instinct that did not care for the effects of time at all.

Pleasure, the sensation of the whole world and one's body as instrument—and this sensation repro-ducing like a crazed amoeba—without prompting or effort even—redounding on itself ad infinitum in gyres of reflection—as when you stand between two mirrors and wave your arms and madness streams its way into the hoary beyonds of imagined space and back to you, without end and without beginning. So, the water on my face. So, the wash of my hands against my face. So the towel, the comb, the toothbrush. So the light against the water that still clung to the tiles. The air across my skin. So, even, the feeling of touching one finger to the other.

I lay on a stone bench in the garden and let the liv-ened breeze dry me off. I found some gin and washed it in my mouth to give my breath the scent of juniper. Then I crawled back into bed and tried to give Jackie what was inside of me. I was virtually limitless.

I do not think it is fair to speak of sex as if it has some kind of universal quality. Saying that sex is a thing unto itself would be just the same as saying that a face, or a voice, is universal and that one face or one voice needs no distinguishing from any other. I sang Christmas carols and it was the same thing, roughly, as singing Carmina Burana. Perhaps. Both are delivered by a choir. But the words are in languages unrecognizable to one another. And Carl Orff had questionable allegiances, especially when compared with the Christ Kind. You could say sex has a universal quality, but to do that you'd have to fuck everything and everyone that ever existed, then fuck yourself from their perspectives. And then perform the act repeatedly, on behalf of everyone who ever lived. So—there is no way to say that sex is anything in particular. There is no way to say anything is anything in particular. But we do say something. At least in my case, we must.

If Dante and Virgil had been alive at the same time—and if Dante had not known ahead of time, as he does in the Comedia, where he was being led—Virgil would have been able to convince his charge that the first circle was really the tipply heights of Heaven, and the two would have gotten marooned there, the divine poem scuttled. They would have remained on that level, and they would have fended off any attempts to convince them that there was a whole Jacob's ladder to Paradise above them. At a certain point in your understanding, it does not matter where you are. You are in a crystal palace locked in a chess match with the lofty eyed spirit of the dead Socrates. Arguably, that chess match is going to last forever. You are going to continuously lose that game, but there is no greater honor in any heaven or hell than to sit in slight discomfort and watch the thoughts spool out of Socrates' skull and become movement. Now, change the intellectual for the physical, and you have that morning's experience with Jacqueline Cerny.

Our surrender was devastating. It was complete. My body was deposited inside of her and hers somehow more impossibly yet no less resolutely inside of me. Our whole guts were exchanged, repurposed and replaced. I do not speak of the physicality of the act, which is more or less grotesque and which is not necessary to describe in a world where so many exemplars are readily available. I mean the echoes we had in the afterlife. We felt ourselves perish in that moment and our souls drift away to parts unknown, and not only did we not care, but we were so far away from caring that the concept of caring or not caring was as remote as the beginning of the universe. We—and I hesitate to say "she" or "I" because there was no distinction. We said something violent referencing the stigmata of the son of God. We uttered a string of—could I call them threats? Threats we uttered at the top of our lungs. Threats of absolution. Threats of acceptance. Threats of love. Then we made good on those threats, we followed them through with proclamations, pronouncement, decrees, bulls. And the experience of life was changed.

We remained in the desert for many days and weeks. Out there we had no concept of the seasons. We lived sometimes off the oranges that grew from the trees in the garden. We combined them with vodka, they gave the perfect nourriture. We clasped together, and when we pulled away from each other we left lakes of tears.

We drove back to Pacific Palisades in the silence of high hopes, and we settled into a domestic routine that held all of life in a balance of exertion and art.

I wrote frantically, for the first time in years. I completed four books all in one heave. Three were books I had outlined but never harnessed the energy to write. One was a sprawling work that I vomited start to finish in little more than a month. I broke myself down with labor to expose my core, the essence, the radix. And Jackie too began to sit opposite herself and to paint increasingly vivid self-portraits. Here we began, without intention and without hesitation, the heartland of our experience. We forgot about everything and everyone else. I looked at Jackie and in her face was written the hieroglyph of my entire life. I took pleasure in things as mundane as plucking the hairs out of my ear. Cleaning the toilets. Beating the rugs. Mopping the floors. Contemplation. I even spent time re-reading my library, which was rare for me—I had not felt the need to absorb other people's thoughts since I had written my tenure monograph, *The Snake Lifter,* five years before. Now just an excuse to remain in Jackie's presence and enjoy, rather than dread, the interference of her monologues, was enough.

"In you I have opened up like a landscape in a hurricane. One of my mothers dug into the earth and planted a locust tree. To her it symbolized that humanity was so sinful that it deserved to be decimated by a plague of locusts. But the tree rooted down and bore terrific fanlike leaves and drew no pests. It scratched its own ancestry on the skies, and it will outlive us by hundreds of years. That is my moral stance. We are part of nature, not apart from it. My voice is no less momentous than Miller's or Picasso's. I am shedding all my throwaway layers, so that the ghost of Pope Joan can leap out of me like a starlet from a human birthday cake. There is no sin or forgiveness. It is all reflection.

"I expected to die of the needle, like my mothers and everyone around them. So, out of curiosity and a distaste for predictability, I never did touch the needle. I touched everything but the needle. I snorted the stuff. I smoked it. But I never touched the needle. So here I am alive, and no clue of how to proceed. If I did have a clue of how to proceed, I would know what there was to come, what would happen to you and to me.

And besides our ultimate demise I have no idea what is even going to happen this next instant, or what it even means to 'happen'. How do we know if an occurrence is over, when it replays itself in our minds so often? And when does an event begin? When did I start to love you? I feel it was long, long before I was born, when I was still the dust fleck of a giant comet breaking off and becoming this family of planets, breaking off and becoming this arm of the galaxy, and getting reeled in by the gravity and the spiraling solar sheets of our yellow dwarf. When did Napoleon cease to exist, when did he stop happening? We still dream of him. His people still roam the earth. Accounts of his destruction and the laws of his making still season the minds of men. For us women, by the way, it must seem so strange to you, it is not Napoleon but Empress Josephine who lectures to us from the pages of history. Marry well, sure, but above all make sure you produce issue. That way, since we ladies rarely achieve immortality through our works—we maintain our mystery as individuals just as we hide our sex from view—we can see our minds and bodies reflected in the eternity of our blood line."

So she sang. And she painted a thousand versions of herself and placed them in every nook and shelf and dead space in the house. In my hours when I was tired of writing I sketched her with my pencil, sometimes from the naked Jackie and sometimes from her naked facsimiles, a thousand times just to see if my reproductions ever could match the form in which I saw her. In one of her poses I was behind her, and I could see between her legs the pulsations of that font of life—and I created a dozen portraits from this angle, each one of them wildly different—just as an entire forest scene will come off differently depending on the openness and hue of its central flower. And that forest scene, on account of its protean form, cannot be possessed, cannot even resolutely be described. And if you approach that forest day after day and try to read its secret language, you realize that the identity of the central flower, if there is such a thing, can change without your ever knowing.

I nonetheless came to master the art of capturing Jackie's poses, and when she saw that my drawing skill had progressed to a level of clarity, she urged me to move on to the far more complex art of sculpture, where one must draw from every imaginable angle. It was in that medium, elbow deep in the primordial clay, that I learned from a whispering Jackie (who had just returned from the post office) that I had won the elusive and mind shatteringly lucrative Frazier Prize for my book *The Origins of Enlightenment*—one of the works I had hastily sketched and composed there in Jackie's presence, in one overheated moment.

"You won that prize, Jacqueline," I said. "It is yours. My work is merely a drawn-out reproduction of your speeches. Take it and buy yourself—I don't know. Buy yourself whatever pleases you. I am beyond the mundane world of dollars and cents. It is telling that in the materialistic world the most important digit is a place holder, a declaration of non-entity, the last and most derelict letter in the alphabet, the definition of nothingness."

"You are far too generous Polonius. I have no words. This is a sum I cannot repay."

"You have already, a thousand times."

"By the way—I forgot, there is a call for you."

"Where?"

"Waiting on the phone."

"Tell them to fuck off."

"It is a he. And the he is your friend, it seems."

"We are occupied here."

"He maybe simply called to wish you congratulations. The least you could do is answer."

I washed my hands in the laundry sink, which with all of our creations had become one of the great abstract art works known to man or woman, and I made my way into the study, where the phone sat face up and alone on the couch. On the side table where the phone's cradle lay, there stood a statue of Jackie in the pose the ancients would use to denote a divine or a semi-divine personage raised from the aquifers of Hades or dropped from the Olympian skies—one arm sinuously raised and the opposite toe curled over the arch of the other foot—a Trajan's column of being that turned about itself like a wave of light in slow motion. When I moved around that statue, the vacant eyes seemed to follow me. This gave me a series of hallucinogenic shocks. And to look upon that pearlescent representation of her naked body made me feel equally naked, to the point of feeling turned inside out. My legs gave way. I lay down on the couch and raised to my ear a reproduction of Federico's voice.

He spoke for a moment. I listened. I tried to speak. I could not. I hung up. My whole body was on fire.

He called back. I did not answer. I knew word for word what he was going to say.

I could see in the study's mirror that my face was so rosy it looked to have been tattooed. I contemplated passing out on the couch and pretending that what I had heard was simply of no consequence. I stared into the eyes of the statue of Jacqueline, who, if art imitated life at that moment, maintained her composure with the utmost grace against forces that threatened the very idea of her existence. I got up. The room tilted haphazardly on its axis. I walked out of the study and through the main rooms to the terrace, where the actual Jackie beckoned me to submerge my hands again in our mountain of clay. She had in the cradle of her lap one of her many copies of Calvino, and her hair draped down just to brush the page. I looked at my hands, which were fading in and out of a veil of atmospheric static, and I applied them to the mountain.

Sculpture, unlike the other arts, gives us a firsthand account of creation. It is not possible to fashion a thing of beauty without taking nature as one's guide. Hence we imagine our god as a spirit in human form—or as a couple—for he—or they—could not have invented us without following their own mirror images in an alpine lake in the crags of Olympus—or without taking each other as guides. If they were sensitive to the distortions of reflections, Juno made man, and Jove made woman, according to their respective visions of one another. They knew they would not get it right at first— they needed practice. Out of gleeful abstraction and an admission of humility, they put a smile on the face of a swimming mammal and gave it their own drive to sex. Then came the birds, the one-word wonders, who gave the gods millennia of distraction and amusement, especially in the crafting and dyeing of feathers, which became an important subset of creativist art. At the point when that art form had become decadent, as seen in the peacock and the penguin, someone decided that something had to be done. Hence the capuchino, or the "monk" monkey—it is hard to see how the gods knew that their earliest human experiment would resemble the mendicant of a later age—but there is much in this story that is hard to see. Jove and Juno created dolphins, peacocks, peregrines, penguins, capuchins without looking at each other or in the mirror. But was the human in fact the pinnacle of their aesthetic achievement? Or are we simply another practice round for something, or someone, else?

Suffice it to say, that it is impossible to create a human figurine out of clay without a model, for the mind cannot hold so much as the dimensions of a finger, let alone a face, without hitting its geometric limit. More the miracle, then, that Jackie and I sculpted a flawless replica of Cherry November from memory—and in Jackie's case, from pure imagination—while staring at each other.

TWENTY-SIX

"THE SORT OF MAGISTERIAL WRITING"

The sort of magisterial writing that claims to know something about beauty and how it is organized, that claims to have an imperial eye into what is high and what is low, and states its case for truth as if a single truth could exist—in other words, any sort of writing that is anything but a straight confession of your sins—is total and entire and incontrovertible trash. Only by means of self-exposure, to the depths of our inner leprosies, may we begin to reveal the upper strata of truth. But I have trodden this ground. I have trodden all grounds.

Our greatest invention as a species is the afterlife. Instead of the mourning monkey, who truly believes that his mother is gone, and wastes away by her fly-eaten body, we place her in Rai, in Wonderland, where she watches over us forever. Every war, civilization, revolution, creed, and dogma claims to know, claims to know and believe, claims to know yet not believe, claims that there is nothing to be known and so belief is quite beside the point, claims that there is nothing to be known and so belief is all there is to be had, claims that knowledge and belief are a distinction without a difference, or claims that knowledge and belief are vacant for there is no use pondering our relationship with a universe that could give less than a hoot about its relationship with us. Gravity is a stevedore that will lodge us in the earth and feed us to the sun. Hence the back of an ambulance resembles a furnace, into which our unwitting bodies are heaved—to be cremated by the insatiate fires of time.

So Turner's body was consumed by that mechanical ghost. One of the medics crouched idly near the plaster head whose expression was vacant, whose expression was final. Cruelly, most cruelly, nothing happened. I reached out for Turner. The feeling was that of reaching for the waters cascading off a precipice and becoming the mist that masked their landing. For God's sake never mind. There was no metaphor for the feeling. My body seized, and I hit the ground. I believe that for more than a minute my heart did not beat. I lay on the cobblestones, and I opened my mouth to the rain. Federico appeared. He tried to pull me off the ground, he was screaming. I felt the mirror images of his strength and voice pull me back to the earth. When it must have become clear to him that he was not moving me, he stood over me like a centurion, stroked his beard, and directed traffic. He bent down from time to time to check my pulse and his watch. He tried to pick me up. I stiffened. He put me back down. He tried again. I stiffened. He put me back down. He waved to one of the medics. I saw him but did not see him. The two men picked me up. I crunched myself into a fetal position, and they put me back down. They compressed me into an aboriginal ball, and rolled me into their arms like a tumbleweed and into the back seat of Federico's car. At that point I started to scream. Not because I had something to communicate through those screams, but because if I did not scream, the force of my own agony would suffocate me. Federico, with such patience as I could not fathom, drove me through the marquis routes of the city. We hit the wide deserted boulevard of Broad Street. We circumnavigated City Hall. We drifted out the Parkway, illumined by the merciful, merciful traffic lights and their toreador cadences, and were released into the serpentine crags of Kelly Drive and its cliffside darknesses. When we reached the Falls bridge, Federico stopped at a gas station to retrieve, of all things, a jug of iced tea. He passed the jug to me and took it back, and passed it and took it back, all the way up Lincoln Drive to the deeply haunted forests of

Wissahickon. We descended the ravine to the banks of the river. Federico idled for a moment. He smoked a cigarette. And he drove us all the way back to the city. He repeated the cycle until I was calm—it must have been about three or four hours, at which point we had imbibed many liters of iced tea. Benevolent loneliness washed over us. The dawn peeked its eye over the corner of the night. I crawled into the front seat to have a look at what the world had borne up. The river and its broad Seurat bank canopied in plane trees was filmed in silver and coated with the rusted hands of leaves left by the first winds of fall. An horizon of cars decorated the opposite bank, from which dusted and industrial misery grew. But even that less artful forest had its faceted charm in this early light—its own just exposed nakedness. When Federico reached the Falls Bridge he crossed it and pushed us up through the city line and down into the streamside roads of Penn Valley that form labyrinths. Down here the road was darkened entirely in a different sort of shade—not deriving from grey or black but deriving from the rich wet oranges of the fallen pine needles and the deepwater blues of the underlying soils and filtered through the teardrops falling from the leafy cathedrals all around us, and the shocked and virginal whites of the birches in their slow parades along the stream sides, one millennium after another. There came an intersection that formed an acute crescent at its hinge—and here a stream flowed through an open copse of conifers and spilled over a makeshift waterfall and over the road. Federico drove through the stream and up a winding embankment. The earth rose up around us as if we were to be engulfed. He pulled off the road and through decrepit arches that guarded an entire hill and its horizons from the world. Over the crest of the hill rose the daunting stone chimneys and turrets and the bleeding leaden glass of an abandoned—what could have been an insane asylum but for the affection with which it had been abbreviated, miniaturized, vanquished, blown to bits, forgotten. Federico pulled off the driveway into an understory of widespread oaks, and he shut off the engine. We stepped out of the car.

I took one step, then another. I looked up and around. Turner's absence hit me from all sides, in a blind suffocation. I fell back against the car. Federico put my head under his arm and held me up and pulled me out into the center of a leaf padded field. After a few eternities I opened my eyes and looked at him.

"I am so tired," I said.

"I know," he said.

"Can we sit down?"

"Yes."

He went back to the car. I teetered there like a marionette without its puppeteer. He returned with some spare clothes, which he lay like a patchwork over the wet ground. We lay down together.

"We are," I said.

"Yes, we are."

"We are some-bodies."

"Yes, we are somebodies."

"We are somewhere too. Somewhere we are."

"Somewhere we are indeed."

"We are somewhere under the rising sun."

"Yes, somewhere, somebodies, under the rising sun."

"Somewhere."

"Yes, somewhere."

"He was innocent, Federico. Innocent he was."

"I know. Yes. He was innocent."

"The meaning of all this is now so garbled that no one will ever find the thread."

"The thread is woven of what you do and what you do not do."

"He will be dispersed, Federico. Dispersed and dis-integrated."

"He will reconstitute, just beyond human view."

"I am so tired, Federico, so tired of pretending there is such a thing as knowledge. I feel you want to do something. I am listening, I am your servant, Federico. I know you want to—and I am trying—I know you want to bring me back to life. In order for that to happen, though. In order for that to happen, I need a transfusion.

A bona fide exchange of my body with another body. Because I am poisoned through and through Federico. Poisoned I am. Poisoned."

I felt so toxic that I needed to tear off my skin. I took my dress off, and the fickle winds of autumn tried but failed to calm my boiling guts. That part of me that remained covered—in those days ladies kept their pubic hair long and flowing as a sign of woman-hood and fertility—I continuously fanned to cool down and I wrenched at the hairs and actually succeeded in pulling out handfuls at once. My brain felt that at any moment it was going to explode in my skull and begin leaking out my eyes and ears. My heart could be seen pounding like a prisoner on the parchment walls of my chest and stomach. I let out little yelps of helplessness as waves of panic built and crashed over me. I had the foreboding feeling that nothing, not relocation or reca-libration or man or substance or meditation or practice would relieve me of such metaphysical withdrawal. Federico placed his hand on my forehead and pushed the matted hair away from my face. He started to speak again, but every word he spoke made me worse. My vision went wavering far out of focus and compre-hension, a force pulled me apart from my own sense of existence. It is said that the shutdown of the body's organs, its measure of self-arrest that withdraws the body from its experience of the truth, is a merciful curtain that falls on the stage of consciousness. But the velvet curtain is heavy, and when it cut through the air of autumn between me and the last hanging leaves of the great-grandfather oaks and made those strong static bodies disappear, I was not ready, Polonius, I was not ready to have my head held down by the hand of Saturn in the river of night. I thrashed about, I fought him, thinking I could still get out, go back. I could not get out or go back.

Federico got clothes back on me, and he brought me into the house. It had been a monastery for a small group of monks who had settled here in the nineteenth century. When I crossed the threshold, the smell of ancient incense leeched from the walls and made me feel like I had been embraced by a Spanish stronghold. Federico fed me, bathed me, wrapped me in towels and cocooned me and slept with his arm over me in a paneled bedroom festooned with faces and wooden and golden crosses and containing a sinful little sink in the corner. He woke me up at dawn and walked me in a state of paralysis through the halls and told me stories about imaginary men who had lived here— and he narrated the hagiographies tessellated in the stained-glass windows and represented in the smoked oil paintings and tarnished icons and the carvings hidden in the woodworks. Saint Sebastian was repre- sented everywhere, his shocked face was repeated in the plates, the doorknobs, the banisters, the moldings, the window cranks. Turner's face was represented in Saint Sebastian, in the faces of all the representations around me, even in the representations of myself in the multitudes of peppered mirrors.

Federico walked me in circles and gyres and labyrinths. He walked me through the decrepit gardens and the blown-out orchards. He explained to me that he was going to let both of those once orderly plots go back to their natural state, and he predicted that in a few decades there would be no trace of human intervention on the landscape, if he exercised enough restraint to leave everything alone.

There was a grass tennis court behind a wall of some sort of box hedge that had grown to such a height that most of the court was dead, it had seen no sun. Federico found two antique rackets and a ball and started lobbing shots at me. I stood there, staring into eternity, and I thought of a recurring dream—this is the remembrance of the remembrance of a dream. I thought of a dream where I stood at a window in my home in Philadelphia, a large window that was larger than any window I really had. Behind me, the house was laid out in a circular fashion, as if the flat earth had been translated into a globe then stretched and laid flat once more. My mind wandered in that fictional land behind me. There were palm trees, and one of my unborn siblings was calling to me from a great height. But never mind . . . . I stood at the window. The world outside was the usual city and its, how should I say, its usual purposes. It was one man walking from one side of the street to the other, and it was another man walking from the other side of the street to the one. It was also a man who stood on the street corner exactly opposite me, but unlike all the other signs of life out there, he stood behind an easel. He looked me in the eye with his electric blues, then he looked back down at the canvas. Back to my eyes, back to the canvas. Back to my eyes, back to the canvas.

I felt a heightened sense of exposure, a sense of being not merely naked but somehow turned inside out, and the sense of being observed so closely made the hairs on my stomach come alive, in fact gave me a shot of what could not be mistaken for anything other than pleasure. In the dream (I don't know what I did in real life at this point, or what real life actually was), I closed my eyes and thought of my mother. Her bright and muddy boots were elevated on the tack table and crossed over one another in the blue light of our little school room. She was smoking, smiling, and speaking to me in a tone that could not be shaken from its joy in remembering Livy's remembrance of Scipio Africanus. She told of his generosity towards his enemy Hannibal, his desire to see the whole world flourish, and how he was not understood during his lifetime, and would never be emulated. For that precarious moment in the dream, I felt the sort of self-fired contentment that my mother seemed to feel at all hours. Then the artist finished, he took the canvas up out of his easel and he showed it to me. This was the moment in my dreams when I was shaken awake—the moment when the artist turned the canvas around and raised it up over his head for me to witness the *cosa impossible*—the truth of me and my place in the world.

—

TWENTY-SEVEN

"ON THE MORNING I LEFT THE WEST"

On the morning I left the West for Philadelphia, the autumn rains were trolling the desert in the holds of great clipper ships in the sky, whose billowing sails cast dark shadows of nourishment on Yuma, on Palm Desert, on Salton City, on Joshua Tree. No sooner had the fleets arrived than they evanesced, leaving the atmosphere with a prismatic fog. Spots of moisture carried little spots of sun, and these gathered on my face and hands so that I appeared decorated in tiny golden telegrams. The roads and the faces of manmade things and objects reflected a scarlet glow that was reminiscent of the evening air on remote islands sculpted by the equatorial trades. In the slipstream of the clippers there emerged, then bloomed, an incandescence of pure nothingness.

I must confess, Antonia, I did not leave Jackie in California. On the trip across the county she was my guide and nightingale and my professor of all things free and numinous. In her company the ride was complete in a single flourish, and it was together that we arrived at Federico's weathered monastery on the outskirts of the city. I remember rain in the air that day too, although it was of the Londoner, the monochromatic sort. Federico, November, and Elise lay in the front field beside burlap sacks full of apples. The grass was matted with the rust of sycamore leaves. The most prepossessing aspect of the property, a grassy-banked brook, traced cursive loops through the trees. The mist was thick with the earth's perfume. We embraced, all of us. November's lips were sticky with the flesh of the apples, and her cheeks were cold papyrus having served so long as a riverbed for her bereavement. As I held her to my chest I felt her ribcage vibrate as if the heart were trying to break free. I opened my eyes and could see that in the background Federico was leading Elise and Jackie away to the house, and he gave me one long receding gaze of gratitude and kind admonition. I held November in my arms all afternoon, all evening, and all night. Her breath was pained, slow, strident, deliberate. She would fall into a shallow sleep and almost immediately awaken herself with horror. Again into sleep, again into horror, again into sleep, again into horror.

In inscrutable tongues heavily peppered with jags of insanity, she sometimes uttered the names of Joseph Turner and Anna Delancey, as if they had died on the same day, in the same fashion, or as if the names were two ways to refer to the same person. I brought wine, I brought whiskey, I brought drugs and more drugs, I brought Elize and Federico and even Jackie, nothing helped. Deep in the night it got worse. Waves of electric seizure ravaged her body. They were born out the base of her skull and built mass and fury as they crashed into her pelvis and rattled her legs. Worse, her condition seemed to be contagious, for in the morning when the sun rose I could barely stand, I felt that all the blood had dropped out of me and pooled in my feet, and my own perception of the world was beginning to waver.

I could not stand, so I did not.

She could not stand either, so she did not.

She could not speak, so I did not speak.

She cried for Turner, so deeply and at such length that all I could do was cry for Turner too. I did not know the man—yet in the embrace of a broken November I loved him, missed him—adored him if only to see the lips of November part to reveal a sound, a smile, a word—a single word—in any language—anything to secure our spirits from puncturing the atmosphere and dissolving in the abyss of space. It was not to be—I gave up my heart to her suffering, and a thousand demons took domicile in my chest—all of whom had something to say about being dead and gone. Not having been dead and gone I had nothing left with which to counter them, no hard evidence that life was anything other than an invitation to disappearance. My body failed to shelter me from eternity—every bone rattled its neighbor—the cumulative vibration threatened to shake my skull off its neck. I tried to scratch my fingernails into an image that would bring me back to life, but all that came to me was creamed corn, whale blubber, Anna under the bridge, Anna on the beach, Anna with a Baltika Seven, Anna in the Sanskrit section—Crowen Steam—the River—Othello. Days later, November finally spoke:

"We never buried her, Polonius."

"How could we have buried her? The river buried her."

"Her family."

"She had no family."

"All the same, we should bury her."

"How?"

She was pulling up her jeans. They were like a parachute on her—we must have slept for weeks—we must have slept for centuries.

"Not bury. Just set free."

November went outside and started gathering wood from the forest edges. Federico, Elise, Jackie and I watched her from the kitchen, and I started to plot the feast that would break our fast. Once November had gathered a pile of deadwood, we found a can of gasoline in the garage and started a fire. In the fiercely animate flames tortured by their own heat, we put Anna Delancey's soul to the winds. It rose in scarlet embers and cascaded back down to earth as ashen snowflakes. I took a sip of wine—how long had I been enclosed, bullied, and raped by sadness?—November gathered more wood—falling ashes everywhere—the fire was becoming a conflagration—somewhere in the changing faces of the fire there flashed the birdlike faces of my dead parents, of my unborn children. November kneeled on the ground, and in unsteady voice proclaimed that the soul of Joseph Turner was now subject to the heat of the flames, which wrestled with him furiously until he, too, was committed to the blue sky.

"Gone," said November. "Let everything be gone and be borne out into the world again. Let all grief, all darkness, all emptiness be yielded up to the fire. Let all fear of what has been and what will be—be yielded up to the fire. Let what remains be the voices of our loved ones, the sweetness of the air, the majesty of nature, the immortality of art—and let the souls of our loved ones be cared for in the afterlife. They no longer belong to us, they belong to the universe. Gone too—is any sense of the tyranny within—the voice of human sacrifice parading as the voice of reason—and gone is the tyranny without—gone are the salesmen, the showmen, the churchmen—let us not speak of them any longer. From now on we only know ourselves and each other—I know only Elise, only Federico, only my dear Jackie—only you Polonius, whom I followed into the icy abyss, for I knew your face from far before the advent of this life—and it is you who said that there is no specific evidence that we ever die—so regardless of the presence of a god we may remain here in faith that another life will open its arms to us—that there are no ends, only beginnings—and so:

"Down here on this wandering jewel, whose eyes do cloud with each passing year, whose once fecund breast desiccates with each repetition, whose emerald hair silvers and grays with exhaustion and ruin—whose skin is torn by a million horsemen with a million scythes—whose air congeals in our lungs—we down here on this saturnine sphere will not lose faith—we will not surrender our souls to the hypothetical savior—the one who would have us keep our legs crossed and our lips shut so that neatly, cleanly, we might be mowed down with the rest. My dear family, of what use is innocence, if it lands us in the same grave as the Hun and the Visigoth? Of what use is innocence in this late hour of our devolution, when our antlers do weigh us helpless and prostrate—and the only true voices issue from a grave placed at Holy Trinity over four hundred years ago? Let us lose all connection with this lost world, and let us imagine how we would feel if the bar-riers in our own psyche were shattered to reveal the unity of time and eternity, the unity of life and death, the unity of body and soul, the union of love and this uncurable pain, and the unity of what we call the good and what we call the evil."

That night we lived thousands of years. We saw and felt the beginning and the end of everything, each in his and her own versions and visions—and the two ends of time were identical in their representation as the fire in front of us that raged, rolled, surrendered to gravity, then finally metamorphosed.

I do not know if the fire became the earth, became the air, became the embers, or did it become the pre-cursor to you, Antonia? Were you given to exist in that moment, in the ecstasy of our suffering? And how did you, at such an early age, come to comprehend the circle that conjoins the greatest loss and the greatest gain, and thereby floats all human souls in the same benevolent embrace—was it the ever-present symbol of untimely death and ultimate sacrifice carved into the facades and supports of all the oldest and most hallowed structures? Was it a message etched in your mother's face when she would lose all bearing in a moment and she would peer out at us as if trapped in another lifetime? Or could it have been the very fact that the "you" of November could become the "I"—the daughter become the mother—and that you could roll back our lives to the very beginning—not by going back, but by going inside? Forever we will fold into and out of each other, like the seas—impossible to parse, impossible to encompass, impossible to measure. I can attest to a private identity: when you were born, I witnessed the first flash your eyes made when they opened into the world—the very same that November's would make when they had witnessed a tone or an image inside of her, and they clamored for an instrument—a brush, a piano, a voice—I beg you, do not let the inevitable, the impending violence stop your mouth.

Antonia—begin!